Gloria's Song

Grandma's Wedding Quilts
Book #11

A Sweet Americana Historical Romance

By

KATHRYN ALBRIGHT

Cover design Copyright © by Shanna Hatfield
Copyedit by Joyce Lamb

ISBN-13: 970-0-0084729-1-1

DEDICATION

Dedicated to my mother, Gloria,
whose love of music has filled my life with
joy.

ACKNOWLEDGMENTS

My humble thanks to the members of **Sweet Americana Sweethearts** – my fellow authors who graciously helped me with the technical side of independent publishing, particularly Kristin Holt & Shanna Hatfield, and to Robyn Echols who had the initial vision for this project. It has been a joy…

THE FLOWER BASKET
QUILT PATTERN

The basket was a symbol of hearth and home, and it was an item that pioneer women used constantly in their daily lives. This motif found its way onto all sorts of things—stoves, ceramics, china, and of course, quilts.

KATHRYN ALBRIGHT

CHAPTER ONE

Barrington, Virginia ~ 1888

Gloria Palmer entered the foyer of the Tarkington Dinner Club on the arm of Mr. George Welbourne III at precisely seven o'clock on Christmas Eve. He handed off his black overcoat, ecru scarf and silk top hat to the waiter, and then eased her velvet cloak with the ermine trim off her shoulders, taking care not to catch it on the sprig of holly he'd pinned to her collar. Tall, dark, handsome and smart, George was perfect in every way. Too perfect—a fact that caused butterflies in her middle when he beamed the entirety of his attention on her.

She took a deep breath, enjoying the fragrance wafting from the boughs of pine draped in garland fashion along the walls and over the entryway. Beyond where she stood, the dining and ballroom area had been decorated with more boughs that were held together at each end by large red velvet bows and a cluster of tiny brass bells.

The bells jingled like mad as the heavy oak door slammed open behind her and a brace of cold, December wind swept through the foyer.

"You cannot enter," the doorman said in his most official tone. He had guarded the door for as long as Gloria had been allowed at the club — ever since her debutant party when she was seventeen. He had always reminded her of a gruff bear. She peered around his portly girth to see who had been so unfortunate as to agitate him.

A young man stood in the entryway. His brown pants, wet from the slush and snow, were plastered to his lower legs. Small dark splotches grew on the shoulders of his woolen coat where the sleet melted into the fabric. He held a stiff paper folder under his arm, securing it against his side with his elbow as he whipped off his worn woolen gloves and flat cap. Wavy blond hair sprang back into place after its recent mashing from the cap.

"I'm Stryker's replacement, tonight. Me name's, Colin McDougal."

"You're late." The doorman looked down his nose. "You're to go around to the back. Take it up with the man there."

Mr. McDougal glanced about at the small audience. "And risk getting my music wet? It's worth a pretty penny. What's wrong with me going through this way?"

"Rules is rules, Irish."

The man's chin jutted up. "Shouldn't commonsense be the rule?"

Gloria thought he had a point, but knew he wouldn't win. The doorman took his job very seriously and had always guarded the entrance as though he were protecting the diners from miscreants of the basest sort.

"You'd best attend to what I say if you want to work in these quarters," he said now, and with a hand to the young man's shoulder, pushed him firmly back through the doorway and out into the light drizzle.

Gloria leaned forward to watch, impressed by the young man's boldness and his attention to his music, and hoped the music wouldn't end up in the slush of the gutter. She would feel the same way about her music pieces, although she would be utterly embarrassed to have an audience and so would meekly obey the doorman to avoid making a scene.

Mr. McDougal stumbled down the two steps. Quickly, he regained his footing and then tucked his folder inside his coat. Giving the doorman a dark look and mumbling something under his breath, he plopped his cap back on his head and strode off into the night.

"Gloria!"

George's voice penetrated her thoughts.

His dark eyes held a glint of amusement. "You dropped your reticule. Was it on purpose?" he chided as though talking to a child. He picked up her property, brushed off a trace of mud from the snow and soot tracked in on the plank flooring, and then handed it back to her. "Are you testing me?"

She looped the drawstrings of the bag over her wrist and refrained from answering. He was only teasing her. It hadn't been on purpose at all. And not a test. Of course, George would pick it up. She had no doubt as to his attentiveness or chivalry toward her. He never dropped things, never faltered. He made her feel at once treasured like a princess and wanting like a child in the same moment.

"Your father is waiting. Come."

Ahead of her, Father led the way to their personal table, the one close enough to the orchestra to enjoy the music and yet a few tables back so that they could still converse with each other easily. Father was dressed much like George, but instead of the more formal black, her father wore a dark gray woolen suit. His sterling silver cufflinks gleamed in the soft light from the gas lanterns as he pulled out the chair for her mother.

"What was that all about, Stephen?" her mother asked. She fingered the double strand of pearls at her neck, a ploy she had explained once to Gloria, meant to draw attention to a long neckline.

"Nothing to worry about, dear," her father answered. "A miscommunication with the help."

George held out her chair for Gloria. "After that display of temper, I doubt he'll find a welcome here. The owner will see to that."

She lowered herself into her seat, sitting slightly askew so that her small bustle did not get crushed at the chair's back. "It was an honest mistake. He obviously has never been here before."

"Any fool knows that musicians—any of the help, for that matter—use the alley door," George said. "I can't imagine that he is much of a pianist anyway. The best ones are German or Russian. Not Irish."

It surprised her that he knew that much about music in the first place. He seldom spoke of it. "You sound as though you dislike the Irish," she said, trying to understand his reasoning.

"I dislike a person who doesn't know his place."

And here she had just thought Mr. McDougal's protest was a means to protect his music, just as he had said. No ulterior motive. No hidden agenda.

It was not the first time George had concluded something so rapidly. His fast-thinking and spot-on decisions in money-matters had attracted her father in the first place. A year ago, Father had retained the firm that employed George as an adjunct financial advisor. Then six months ago, impressed with George's capabilities, he had offered him a lucrative position within the Davis Shipping Company and George had accepted. That he was an ambitious man, she had no doubt. Still, for him to have so little compassion toward others less fortunate seemed uncharitable, especially on a night such as this.

"Of all nights there should be music on Christmas Eve," she murmured, then brightened as a bit of inspiration gripped her. "I suppose, if he doesn't play tonight that I could take his place."

Her mother gasped. "Good heavens, Gloria!"

George chuckled. "A Palmer? Performing in a dinner club? You are only saying that to stir up your mother."

"I know several Christmas songs," she said defensively. "What is the difference between playing here or at Marlowe Hall?"

George took her hand. "Very amusing. Your talent at the piano far exceeds anything needed here."

"Your tutor said that you needed a break," Mother said. "Time off over the holidays."

"With only seven weeks left before the audition, I mustn't stop. And Mr. Peers is more interested in helping his son win the competition than he is helping me. For that reason, I am hesitant to follow his advice."

George released her hand and sat back in his chair. "When did you hear this?"

"Yesterday. I ran into his son, Joseph, at Sharrell's. I've been meaning to tell you Father, but you were home late last night and then early to the office today."

"That does sound like a conflict of interest," Father said slowly, frowning slightly. "Is that how you see it, George?"

The waiter arrived at that moment and began explaining the special offerings that evening. "For drinks, will you be having the usual, sir?"

"With your permission," George said quickly, intervening before her father could answer. "Tonight, I hoped to have a small celebration. I'd like to order champagne."

The waiter looked to Father for confirmation. He nodded and then squeezed her mother's hand.

"I only wish Theodore were here to celebrate with us," Mother said softly.

Gloria glanced around the table. Her mother seldom spoke of her brother. "Just what is it that we are celebrating?"

George placed a small, white box, tied up with a red velvet ribbon, in front of her. "Our engagement."

Colin gripped his collar tight and headed toward the alley. He had been sorely tempted to leave after that comeuppance, except for the fact that he owed his friend a favor…and he needed the money.

His father didn't see the need to pay him for working at the pub, seeing as how the money would just go back into the money jar to support the family. It was the extra Colin earned through his music that was his to use as he wished.

The tall, thin man who opened the back door took one look at Colin and pulled him inside. "Been waitin' for you. Heard you play once at McDougal's. I'm Frank."

At least it was a warmer welcome than Colin had received from the other doorman. Colin removed his cap, rolled it up and stuffed it in his coat pocket. He followed Frank down a narrow, dark hallway until he came to the kitchen. The room was warm with the heat emanating from two large ovens and with the bustle of four cooks. A sheen of sweat coated their pink faces while they performed their tasks. One arranged food on gilt-edged plates, another sliced a roast hot from the oven, and another filled crystal mugs. The aroma of roasting meat and vegetables and hot apple cider and cinnamon reminded him that he hadn't eaten since his late breakfast. His stomach growled.

On a row of vacant chairs, he opened his folder and spread out his music.

"The piano is that way," Frank said, roughly. He indicated a door where waiters streamed in and out constantly, and through which, when opened slightly, Colin saw the dining room.

Colin turned back to his sheet music, looking over each piece carefully. "I want to make sure it isn't damaged from the rain." It wasn't his. He would need to get it back good as new to the music shop before the store opened in the morning. Tamara could lose her job if her boss found out that she let him borrow it.

"No time for that. You're late enough as it is." The doorman tugged at the collar on Colin's coat. "You can't wear this."

Colin braced himself as the man peeled off his coat and hung it on a nearby peg. After seeing the fancy clothing of those in the dining area, he felt underdressed even though he wore his Sunday best. He smoothed his tie and tucked his shirt in at his waist again.

The doorman eyed him critically. "Anyone tell you this is a quality establishment?"

"I heard it was a gentleman's club."

"Long time ago. Now it's for fine dining, and on special occasions like this here holiday we have select benefactors in for private parties. Did you bring a jacket?"

In other words, Colin should have dressed up more. "Do you see one? This is as good as I have."

"Maybe Tom left his."

"Tom's won't fit even if you do find it. And I can't play if I'm constrained."

Frank sighed as if he was the one who had to endure so much. "I'll introduce you. Then start with something lively."

Colin gathered his sheet music and nodded gamely, following Frank to the dining hall. He settled himself at the Fischer grand while Frank walked up to the front of the stage.

"In the stead of Tom Stryker, who is our usual pianist, I'd like to introduce Colin McDougal at the piano."

Colin stood up and bowed to the diners and then realized most of them had returned to chatting among themselves. So much for his grand entrance. He placed his hands on the keys and started with Good King Wenceslas. Tom had warned him to tone down his usual playing style that he used at the pub. The patrons of the dinner club preferred the music to be a low undercurrent to their conversation unless something to dance to was requested. As long as he got paid, Colin would play however they wanted — even upside down and standing on his head. But tonight, being Christmas Eve, he figured he'd insert several traditional carols.

As he played, he glanced up every now and then and looked about the room. He'd never played in such a large room. The acoustics beat those at the pub by one hundred percent. He could also hear the clink of fine china, along with the rustle of long silk dresses and the low hum of conversation. What did these rich and cultured people have to talk about? Their next plan to ruin an honest business like

McDougal's Pub? Best not to go there with his thoughts. His bitterness might leech through into his tunes. He continued playing through his entire repertoire of music.

An hour later, before his break and just to wake them up, he played one of his own.

It was peppy, snappy, and in a few places nearly a march. He glanced around the room to see how the diners reacted. About a quarter of them were listening—that was a change. His gaze collided with that of a young woman sitting at a table halfway back. She looked…attentive. And she was very pretty and polished in her appearance. At the pub, he would have winked and thrown her a quick grin. Not here though.

He finished with an *allesandro* glide and a strong chord, showing off just a little. All in good fun. Then he rose from his seat and gave a quick bow. He looked once more at the woman to gauge her reaction, and stifled a smile. By her expression, he'd shocked her a bit. Probably a good thing that she didn't know the lyrics he had in mind for the piece— nothing too wild—just fun. The men at the pub would enjoy them, but the present audience appeared much too highbrow to appreciate them.

From the side of the stage, Frank motioned to him. Colin followed him back into the kitchen, when the doorman swiftly turned on him.

"What was that at the last?"

"Some of my music."

"Well, don't show off like that again. It's not the sort that is played here. Understand?"

Colin let out a long slow breath. He was just trying to liven the place up a bit. Some of the songs had sounded like those played at a funeral. Even the carols had had more pep. "Yeah. I understand."

"Stick to the normal stuff if you want to get paid tonight." Frank indicated a lone table. "The cook set out a plate for you."

Colin slid into the chair and wolfed down the fish and greens, barely taking the time to taste them, and then washed them down with a glass of water. While he ate, the staff switched from cooking to washing and drying dishes.

When finished, he handed off his plate to them and then walked over to the alley door, wondering if the sleet had changed to rain or snow in the two hours he'd been inside. Pushing the door open, he stepped out. The clouds had moved on and now stars studded the night sky and a full moon cast a bluish tint to the cobblestone at his feet. He dragged in a deep breath of fresh air—crisp and cold. The brick establishments bordering each side of the narrow alley were darkened, but lights streamed through the narrow windows on the second and third floors here and there.

A carriage drawn by a pair of matching white horses pulled up to the end of the alley.

Colin watched as the driver hopped down and placed a box at the door to use as a step. An older man helped a woman up and then entered behind her. The other couple stood to the side, deep in conversation. When the young woman looked right at Colin, he recognized her as the one who had been listening to his last song. She said something to the man beside her that carried to him. "Please, George."

The man, dressed to the nines, didn't sound happy. He helped her into the carriage, then turned, striding a few steps toward Colin. "You there! The Palmers would like a word with you."

The Palmer family…hmm. They owned Davis Shipping and half the wharfs on this side of the Potomac. What could they possibly want with him?

He walked up to the carriage where the older man leaned out the open window. "Good evening. I'm Stephen Palmer. My daughter would like to know the name of that tune you played at the last."

Colin glanced over the others until he came to a younger version of the woman that sat next to Palmer. A quiet intelligence sparked in her eyes. He thought they might be green—or perhaps blue, considering her auburn hair—but in the dark interior of the cab, they looked black.

He bowed slightly. "No name, Miss. Not yet anyway."

"I don't underst—" The confusion cleared from her face. "Then…you mean you wrote it?"

"That's what I said." He raised his chin. She could believe him or not. The two old buzzards who had tried to buy out the pub from under Da, had soon found out that McDougal's didn't cower to a man because of his money.

The man who had fetched him narrowed his gaze.

Guess he could have been a bit more accommodating to the lady, but he'd had his fill of people looking down at him. It still smarted that

New York had rejected this last piece of music he'd sent them. Any interest this woman showed in it couldn't salvage the sting of that disappointment. She probably didn't know all that much about his type of music anyway. He set his jaw. "Is that it, Miss? I should get back. My break is over."

"I'm sorry if I offended you. It's just...I've never met a composer before."

Her apology surprised him. And she'd called him a composer? He huffed out a breath. Wouldn't the boys at the pub have a time with that? They would laugh him out of the city. "It was just a little ditty, miss. Something lively to fill the last few minutes before my break."

"Well, I enjoyed it...and your performance tonight."

Performance? He just played tunes. That's all. She made it sound like he was a show-off. Her way of describing things amused him—making him sound grander than he was. Is that how the rich held themselves apart? Just used different words? It was interesting how she pictured him. But he didn't have time for this. He had to get back and start his second set of songs. "Good night, miss."

Her escort climbed into the carriage and shut the door. Mr. Palmer wrapped his cane on the ceiling of the conveyance, and in quick response, the driver snapped his whip over the pair of trotters.

Colin watched the carriage disappear around the corner, amazed that the daughter of the great Mr. Palmer had made a point to tell him that she liked his music. When the last sound of hoof-beats faded away on the cobblestones, he turned and headed back to the club.

CHAPTER TWO

"Time for the morning run, Colin-me-boyo."

Colin grimaced at Da's intrusion. *Boyo*—his da would never stop calling him that, no matter that he was twenty-four now. He had wanted to finish the last stanza on his new piece before starting work. He gave up, flipped his pencil down and pushed back from the piano. He stretched, relieving the tension in the muscles of his upper back. Served him right for hunkering over the ivories for so long, but early morning was the only time he could work on his music without customers interrupting him. He gathered up the papers and stuffed them back in the cardboard case and then stored it above the cupboard of beer mugs. "Where's Jamie?"

"Off to market for your ma. He'll be back in time for the rounds."

Colin grabbed his apron from the peg and slipped the loop over his head, then tied the thin waist string behind him. He filled a large pitcher from the beer tap, and then began filling the mason jars Da had set out on the counter for the first run of the day. Since the age of eight he had 'made the rounds' to the workers in the warehouses along the docks, taking mason jars filled with brew to them on their morning and afternoon breaks. It was a time-honored tradition...not to mention a boon for his family's business since many of the men would stop off at the end of their workday for a pint with friends before heading home. The task had been handed down to his younger brother when Jamie turned ten, but Colin still filled the jars.

While he worked, his younger brother returned from the store with his mother and headed up the stairs with their purchases. By the time Jamie returned, Colin had topped off the last foamy jar and set it in the wooden tote rack, and then covered it all up with cheesecloth.

"All set."

His brother grabbed the rack and headed out.

Colin looked over the room critically, taking in the differences of a small place like this compared to the dinner club he'd played in a week ago. The row of dark oak tables ran from the front of the pub facing the street to the back room, parallel with the long bar. Both gleamed with Ma's polish — including the nicks and dents. The sunlight shone through the leafless branches of the dogwood out front, through the windowpanes at just the right slant to turn the end of the bar a golden honey color. A wreath on the front door and two on the long wall were the extent of Ma's decorations for the season. He'd have to take those down soon with the holidays coming to a close.

He loved this place and the home his mother and father had made on the second story over the pub. If only Uncle Doug were still alive to enjoy it. His uncle had been the first in the family to come over from Ireland. Once he had established a foothold working at Gunter's Tavern, he'd sent money for Da to come. They'd saved up and a few years later they had gone in together and bought this pub.

That was twenty years ago. Colin, James, and their cousin Patrick, grew up in the bustle and commerce of Barrington's river district. Colin had a good life. He had plenty to eat and knew where his next meal came from. His clothes, although not the cut of Stephen Palmer's, were serviceable and suited him just fine.

So why was he restless lately? He had noticed the feeling before, as it shifted beneath the surface of his daily comings and goings, like a fish swimming back and forth in the waters of the Potomac. It had grown worse when Patrick took off after his row with Da last summer. Since then, more and more responsibility had shifted to his own shoulders and he'd had less time for his music. It was as if a shadow chased him, and playing the piano or writing a new song seemed to be the only thing that held the shadow at bay.

He'd been paid well for that one night of work at the dinner club and he hadn't missed much at the pub. Da and James had closed early and attended Christmas Eve Mass with Ma. He couldn't remember the last time he'd missed Mass with his family and he felt a stab of guilt at that.

He shook his moodiness off. He had work to do to prepare for tonight. New Year's Eve was one of their busiest nights of the year. He hefted the empty keg onto his shoulder and strode to the back-storage room where he set it in the corner. Then he horsed a full barrel down from the ones stacked against the wall and carried it on his shoulder back to the keg rack. He inserted the spigot and tested it for use, hardly aware of the motions that he'd done a thousand times since he was strong enough to lift a keg.

Two hours later, his brother returned and found him in the back room unloading the supply wagon of newly purchased barrels. James set down his rack of empty jars. "There's a man out front asking for you."

Colin immediately stopped whistling. Something about James' tone caught at him. He walked to the edge of the wagon and gave his brother a hand up. "I take it he's not one of our regulars."

"Not by the way he's dressed. He'd be more likely to frequent Watermans on Fifth Street than come here."

Colin immediately tensed. Waterman's was a high-class gentlemens' club on the other side of the trolley tracks. His gut twisted inside as he thought of how Da had nearly lost the pub only six months ago to one of the men there—a man who was ambitiously buying up all the businesses on the street. The wound was still fresh with all the McDougals. If whoever waited for him in the front room was one of those men, he'd find it hard to be civil, but that is exactly what he had to be. "Is it...?"

"Never saw him before," James said quickly.

Colin blew out a breath. "Guess I better go see what he wants." He eased himself off the wagon.

"Was that a new tune?" James asked.

"Trying to work out the chorus." Seemed a new melody always popped into his head when he was busy at work. Something about the mindless physical labor that set his thoughts free. Suddenly, he'd be humming something new. It was annoying when he couldn't take the time to grab pencil and paper to capture it.

James grabbed the next barrel and handed if off to Colin.

He stored it with the others by the wall, and then wiped his hands on his apron. Just knowing the man was wealthy had him on edge. He could take whatever snobbery another man might dish out, but he couldn't stand to have his family hurt. They had worked hard to make a go of this place. A man used to more of everything—like Mr. Gunter, who had a fancy rosewood bar instead of one of solid oak and cushioned chairs instead of wooden stools—might look down his nose, but the McDougal family had nothing to be ashamed of and wouldn't be bullied into trying to sell like the many other businesses on the street.

Colin strode through the doorway into the pub.

At the far end of the bar stood a thin man in a well-cut suit, his overcoat slung over his crooked arm. He hadn't removed his bowler hat. Colin took that to mean he would not be staying for a glass of ale.

Colin stopped before him. "I hear you are lookin' for me?"

The man looked him up and down. "Are you the one who played piano at the Tarkington Dinner Club last week?"

"Christmas Eve, I did. But it's Tom Stryker who works there regular. Are you sure you're not looking for him?"

"I'm sure." The man held out a card with embossed lettering and an address. "I'm Charles Ross. Mr. Palmer requests your presence at his residence."

Colin recalled the one time he'd spoken to the man at the entrance to the alley...or more truthfully, he remembered the man's daughter. Anyone as pretty as that was hard to forget. And he supposed it helped that she liked his music. "What's this all about?"

"You will find out when you arrive."

"I can't make it today. This place will be filling up soon. Tomorrow?"

"The family will be out tomorrow for the New Year's Day festivities. They will expect you the following day—Wednesday at one o'clock."

Guess that would get him back in time to help Da with the after-work crew.

Mr. Ross leaned forward and lowered his voice, so that the few patrons in the pub did not over hear him. "I advise you to leave the apron here." He spun on his heel and left.

Colin smoothed his thumb over the raised lettering on the card. What could Mr. Palmer want with him?

CHAPTER THREE

Gloria paced the length of the solarium, the heels of her shoes clicking on the tile floor as she moved from one tall window-paned wall to the next. "I feel as though I am being punished because Father let Mr. Peers go."

Mother sat at her writing desk with a profusion of ferns and flowering lilies surrounding her, while she penned a letter to the Barrington Women's Club. With a sigh, she set down her silver fountain pen. "You understand he had no choice. Mr. Peers was the one acting questionably. It was fortunate you discovered his situation when you did. However, I'm not sure that this grasping at straws at the last minute—"

"Meaning this Mr. McDougal?"

"Well, dear. The idea of his being able to help this late in your endeavor is a bit preposterous, don't you think? I am befuddled as to your father's decision to hire him."

"And why he waited until the last moment before leaving for the office this morning to tell us." Gloria sighed. It *was* preposterous to think that a club pianist could help prepare her. For certain, he had been enjoyable to listen to and that one composition had caught her ear...but it was going to take a miracle to get her ready for the audition in time and he simply wasn't it. The other pianists vying for a spot at the conservatory had been practicing for at least six months by now. She might have had a chance if only Mr. Sharrell at the music store could have found a professional teacher. But it seemed no man wanted to uproot his life for a total of six weeks' work and then be done with it.

"He'll be here any moment," she said. "I'll go through with it...at least for today, but I intend to bring this up after supper tonight with Father."

"Had you agreed to Mr. Welbourne's proposal, none of this would have happened. We would have been planning your wedding now."

"You already had that planned out," Gloria said, tolerantly. "All the way down to the place cards with their silver holders and etched initials. Sometimes I think it should be you and George getting married."

"Gloria!"

"Well...you and he like so many of the same things. He is always considering how he will make his next profit and you"—she smiled— "you are always dreaming of how to spend it."

Mother flushed slightly. "I do no such thing. It is improper for a woman to speak of money. I simply...listen. Besides, I don't see you complaining about your home and your piano which are the end results of that type of ambition."

She blew out a breath, considering her mother's words. "I would hate to give up my piano. Still, I cannot picture Grandmother Mary's quilt ever looking right displayed in a home of George's. I've never seen George's apartment, but if his office is any indication, his room is probably white and gray. And the quilt is so warm and colorful."

"Such a minor detail to be concerned about. Perhaps you could use it in the servant's quarters."

"It's a wedding quilt! It is supposed to be in my room! On my bed!"

"Dear…quilt or no quilt, you can't make a better match for yourself from the eligible bachelors here in the city. George would take care of you in grand fashion. You could have ten quilts if you wish. Mary's quilt…is just a quilt. You'd…figure something out with it."

Gloria held back the urge to stamp her foot. That quilt was a symbol of love, stitched in love and blessed. Father had brought it back from the ranch a year ago. Hers and Tad's were the very last ones that Grandmother Mary had made before her eyesight started to fail. Ever since Grandmother Mary had finished it, it had been packed away for safe-keeping until her wedding day.

"Please dear. Do sit down. You are giving me a headache with all your pacing." Mother rubbed her temple and sighed. "You certainly are Stephen's daughter at times like this."

Gloria had heard it all before. Whenever she did something her mother didn't approve of, it was because her father's blood coursed through her veins. Of course, Mother had admitted once that it was his coarse ambition and quick wit that had attracted her to him in the first place. Yet for Gloria to exhibit any part of it...She sighed. No matter how hard she tried to act the lady, she always came up wanting in the eyes of her mother.

Her grave impropriety, this time, was that when George had finally asked her to marry him, she had hesitated. Up until that moment her focus had been on auditioning for the Marlowe Conservatory of Music. If she'd said yes to George right then and there on Christmas Eve, a spring wedding would be expected. Planning would ensue...planning that would wrench her time and attention away from her practice for the audition.

Mother simply couldn't understand. Her entire focus had been on finding a suitable husband for Gloria. When George accepted his new position within Father's firm six months ago, Mother had delighted in playing matchmaker. To Mother, Gloria's music was simply a nice accomplishment, something that was meant to help secure a suitable match. Music was nothing that should get in the way of marriage, especially marriage to a man like George Welbourne III.

Gloria continued to pace, pulling her thoughts back to the task at hand and the visitor they were expecting. "This will amount to a wasted afternoon when I could have been practicing."

Mother closed her eyes, the way she always did when Gloria brought up the competition. Then she rose and walked over to her and grasped her hands. "I thought you felt something for George."

"I do. He's...perfect." But what did he really expect in a wife? And could she truly live up to it? If he looked for someone to constantly attend parties with him—or worse, host the parties—she wasn't sure she could measure up. The thought tightened her chest and gave her a headache.

The solarium door opened and Clara, their maid stepped into the room. "Miss Emmeline? Miss Gloria? The young man has arrived."

Mother held out a sealed envelope for Clara. "See to it that you leave this, name down, on the table at the front door. I will mention it to Mr. McDougal after I have a chance to speak with him."

Clara curtsied slightly, took the envelope, and disappeared back into the house.

"What was that?" Gloria asked.

"A small stipend for his time should he agree to our request."

Gloria felt a moment of panic. Her father's idea was laughable. As far as she knew from speaking with the owner of the Tarkington Dinner Club, this Mr. McDougal usually played in a tavern! How good could he really be? How could he teach her anything? The man would probably think the entire thing was as ludicrous as she did and turn on his heel to spread the word that, for a society girl, Gloria Palmer was as strange as they came.

Instead of meeting him, she wanted to retreat to her room.

But she must face this. Certain social expectations came with being a Palmer, her mother constantly said. This was one of them. Graciousness in the face of certain embarrassment, all brought about because of her father. Since her debutant party two years ago, he had become more distant, letting her mother oversee her education as to the finer points of being a lady. She was sure of his love. It wasn't that. But why had he chosen now to meddle? For someone who had participated very little in her life of late, Father had picked a most inopportune time to pay attention. Perhaps she should feel grateful. At least it meant he still noticed her.

To appease her father, she would endure Mr. McDougal for an hour. After that, she could dismiss him and justify it to her father that his plan had failed. After all, Father knew little of the arts. He'd had precious little time for such things while growing up on a cattle ranch. He would believe whatever she said about Mr. McDougal's playing ability.

She barely recalled the man's face. His hair — on the longish side with a bit of a wave — was a dark blond, the type that lightened with streaks of gold in the summer sun. The one other thing she remembered was that he'd had a presence about himself when he'd challenged the doorman to let him enter the club. More than that, his piano playing had drawn her in without the slightest effort. Even ballads and carols she'd heard before had sounded different in the way he nuanced his notes. At the time, it had intrigued her.

Too bad, Father thought it more than it was. She had felt his gaze upon her — searching, calculating — at one point as she listened to Mr. McDougal.

She blew out another breath. It would all be over soon.

She squared her shoulders, walked over to the settee and positioned herself so that she could rise gracefully when he entered the solarium.

"Come with me, sir."

Colin whipped off his cap and followed the housekeeper down the wide, but dark hallway. On either side of the hall, arched doorways revealed rooms as big as the pub. To the right, a library was filled with books from ceiling to floor. To the left was a man's study. More books. A globe of the earth. And a case of old rifles and swords, polished until the handles and blades gleamed. So this was what the rich dallied with in their free time.

He didn't have much free time.

The housekeeper came to a door of glass panes that allowed light to brighten that end of the hallway. She opened it and announced him. "Mr. Colin McDougal." Then she stepped back so that he could pass.

As he stepped into the room he smelled the heavy scents of flowers and rich earth, and felt the more humid weight to the air. The solarium, the housekeeper had said. He'd never heard of such a room. On two adjacent walls, winter sunlight streamed through large windows that looked out onto a large side-lawn covered with snow that stretched down to the river where a stand of pine and maple trees stood.

Large ferns cascaded from hanging pots in three corners of the room. More ferns sat here and there along the walls, along with a small desk which held an inkpot, several pens in a jar, and stacked blank paper. What a great place to write songs! In the center, on a wicker settee, sat two women who looked like older and younger versions of each other. Both were auburn-haired beauties.

He bowed.

The older woman stood. "I am Mrs. Palmer and this is my daughter, Miss Palmer. Please have a seat." She indicated a wicker chair nearby. "May I offer you refreshment, Mr. McDougal?"

"No." He sat down. Then he amended, "No, thank you."

"I'm sure you are wondering why we have asked you to come here."

He glanced at the younger woman. She studied him intently, even as she held herself aloof and quiet, sitting there in her ice-blue dress. "Yes, ma'am."

"We enjoyed your performance at the club on Christmas Eve."

"Glad to hear it. I was helping out my friend."

"Yes. It took us a while to track you down since he was away on holiday."

So, the club had covered up for Tom. His friend was often on a 'holiday.' "Well, you found me. What's this all about?"

"It's a bit...unusual." For the first time, Mrs. Palmer's poised expression faltered. Whatever 'it' was, they were uncomfortable talking about it.

"Just out with it," he said, hoping to encourage her. He'd say the same to his own mother, but here, he wasn't sure what was considered appropriate.

They were so stinking rich. There were probably invisible rules he knew nothing about.

A frown of disapproval darted across the older woman's face, confirming his thoughts.

"All right then. My husband—"

"Mother. Allow me," the younger Miss Palmer said quickly. "The way you played the piano at the club on Christmas Eve caught my father's attention. I'm sure you remember that he spoke with you from the carriage."

He remembered all right. But in his mind, *she* had been the one more interested in his playing. "Yeah," he answered carefully.

"Father thought it might be beneficial for me to assess your technique at the piano—just for an hour—and possibly garner some tips to improve my playing."

He raised his brow. "Technique? I'm not sure..."

"I want to understand your process at the keyboard," she said quickly.

What was she talking about? His process? He just sat down and played. That's all there was too it.

"I've had years of lessons. I should be able to spot your technique without difficulty and appropriate what will work for me."

He snorted softly, finding the way she spoke amusing. "You mean like a beer master giving away his brewing secrets for nothing in return." His cousin, Patrick, would have a time with that one. A brewers' recipe was his signature of the craft.

Miss Palmer blinked, obviously shocked at his bluntness. "I suppose that is one way to look at it." Then her pretty, green eyes narrowed. "I see that you find this humorous. Let me assure you...it is not."

So, this princess wanted something from him. Interesting. She was being careful with her words, as though she had to maintain control of everything going on.

"If you ask me, it sounds foolish."

She stiffened. "You might learn something from me as well."

Most likely he would, but he would never admit it. Not to her. "I do all right on my own."

"So, you are not interested?" She stood up quickly, relief smoothing out the lines above her brows. "Very well. Then I am sorry to have wasted your time and I'll show you out."

He rose to his feet, surprised to find that he was suddenly reluctant to leave. Guess he hadn't charmed her. He'd been on the defensive since he'd arrived, when by most counts, he was a decent fellow.

"Now wait, Gloria," Mrs. Palmer said, standing also. "You've hardly given Mr. McDougal a chance. You know your father will expect more. You need to give the young man that much."

"I'm sure he has other things to do."

It was like watching a game of table tennis and he wasn't all that sure who he'd like to see win. He wasn't sure he had any secrets to offer, but maybe something could come of this better than a wasted afternoon. The young Miss Palmer, although as cool as an iceberg, was an interesting woman. "You said before that this would be like sharing techniques. What would I get in return?"

"We have every intention of compensating you for your time today," Mrs. Palmer said, and then added, "*Monetarily.*"

That last brought him up short. "You are saying...you're going to pay me?" They probably had a grand piano. A nice one. What he wouldn't give to hear one of his own songs played on a really good piano. The one at the pub was in a constant state of needing tuning no matter how much he worked with it.

"Yes. Whatever you made at the club on Christmas Eve. How's that?"

"For an hour of playing the piano?" It was generous. And he could use the money. It didn't take him more than a second to decide. "Sure. I'll do it."

Miss Palmer's eyes widened and she turned to her mother, shutting him out. "This is absurd! You actually expect me to go through with this, Mother? With him? It's embarrassing!"

"Only as far as it will appease your father. Nothing beyond that. You'll remember I hoped you'd forget the entire thing and agree to the engagement."

Colin clenched his teeth, no longer amused. He didn't care to be talked over as though he was invisible. "I've got work to do back at the pub." He took a step toward the door.

Miss Palmer glared at him.

An in that instant, he noticed a moment of defeat in her eyes. Between her mother and him, she didn't stand a chance. And there was something else — a vulnerability that hadn't been there before. It tugged at him. She was tied up in knots about something and it went beyond an hour of 'swapping secrets' over a piano.

"What can it hurt, Miss Palmer? It could be fun." He threw the words out, a soft challenge. He knew the last was a bit cocky but hey, it was a chance to play on a piano that probably didn't have any chipped keys and stayed in tune.

"Fun? Just what are you suggesting?" she said.

Clearly the woman wasn't playing the piano correctly if she didn't have fun with it. "Nothing more than that. Let's see your piano."

She drew in her breath, still glaring at him. Then she squared her shoulders. "One hour. Mother? I'm able to handle this. I'll keep the door open."

"Then I will listen from here. I have correspondence to attend to." She turned to him. "It's been...a pleasure meeting you."

He ignored the hesitation in her voice and bowed slightly. "Ma'am."

Miss Palmer pressed her lips together. "Please follow me to the music room."

Guess his manners didn't impress her.

She moved at a fast clip down the hallway, her head high, her back rigid, not bothering to look back to see if he came to heel. The woman needed to learn how to relax...or smile. He did enjoy the swish, swish, swish of her long, pale blue dress as she marched ahead of him. Her head barely bobbed with her strides, and he wondered if she'd practiced that with books on her head. Tamara had told him once that society girls did that to practice their walk. At the time they had both had a good chuckle over it. He smiled at the thought of Miss Palmer practicing her walk in that way.

She stopped before double-doors, threw them open with a flourish, and then swept into the room. "I'll open the drapes. In the winter, we keep them closed to retain the warmth. I...have difficulty playing well when I am chilled."

He stepped into the room. It was cast in shadows of gray. By the echoing sound of his footsteps he could tell it was large.

Miss Palmer drew aside the heavy drapery on one floor-to-ceiling window and secured it with a sash. Golden light streamed into the room and he realized the walls were a creamy white color. She moved to the opposite side of the window and did the same, her movements graceful. He found himself watching her as she moved on to the next window and wondering what tune he could play to make her unwind.

As more light came into the room, he began to notice details. An intricate, parquet floor. Marble busts of men — six of them. Three lined one side of the room and three lined the opposite side. Six rows of chairs, all facing the piano. She gave performances? In here? She must really be an accomplished musician. He swallowed. What had he gotten himself into?

"How long have you been playing?"

"Eight years. I asked for a piano for my twelfth birthday."

"I thought girls asked for ponies."

"Not me. You may warm up if you wish."

So much for getting to know each other.

The piano stood at one end of the long room. A Sohmer Grand! He'd figured that it would have to be a pricey instrument in a house like this where expense was no option. He walked over and skirted around it running his hand over the smooth surface of the mahogany and rosewood. He'd never seen a more beautiful piano. Elegant carvings decorated the sides and the thick, turned legs. Reverently, he lifted the top, angled it, and positioned the brace. Inside, the strings were pristine. Not a speck of dust. He moved around and sat down at the bench seat, then carefully folded back the lid. The ivory keys gleamed up at him. Clean. Not sticky or dirty like they'd often get at the pub. This was one thoroughbred of a piano.

"What are you waiting for?"

He looked up, slightly embarrassed to find that the room was filled with light and that Miss Palmer had come up behind him. Even though they were away from the solarium he noticed that the faint scent of flowers still clung to her.

"Just taking it all in. I haven't played on something this…grand before. And here it sits for you to use any time you have the itch to play."

"Seems you've changed your tone, Mr. McDougal." Her voice had softened. "You were quite full of bluster in the solarium with my mother. You indicated this would be fun."

There was a hint of blue in her eyes that he hadn't noticed before. Her eyes were shadowed by dark lashes. Pretty, intelligent, impatient eyes.

"It will be."

He stretched his fingers over the keys. "From the looks of this room, this house, I have a feeling you play a different sort of music than I do."

"Try the one you said you wrote."

He was surprised she remembered. Meeting her gaze, he noted the skepticism there. She still didn't believe he'd composed it. "It's not finished. And it's still a bit rough."

"Then play what you have."

He ran the fingers of his right hand up the keys and then back down. The first sounds came through clearer than any he'd ever heard, the bass robust and resonant, the tenor rich and warm, and the treble pure as bells. They absorbed into his skin, into his being.

"Why did you stop?"

Her irritated tone broke through his concentration. Seemed she was intent on getting through this hour and being done with it.

"Do you not hear it?" Couldn't she put aside her impatience for a minute and enjoy the sheer beauty of the sound?

"Please, Mr. McDougal." She tapped her foot.

He stood and walked to the rows of chairs, picked one up and brought it back, positioning it so that she could sit next to the piano. "I'll do better if you don't hover over me."

Her brow furrowed. "Thank you."

He began playing again. It wasn't long before the room faded away and the notes lifted him up to another plane where all that existed was music. He didn't think about the notes or the placement of his fingers or Miss Palmer. All that existed was the

35

music. This particular tune he'd written because it reminded him of his cousin Shannon — innocent, bubbly, and sweet. He finished that tune and segued into another, this one a traditional hymn — *How Great Thou Art*. When he came to the last note, he held the chord until the room was once again quiet.

He sat there, still hearing the richness of the tones reverberating inside him. It took him another few seconds to come back to himself. Slowly, the surrounding sounds of the day permeated his mind — a crow cawing outside the window and the tic-toc of the grandfather clock at the far end of the room.

With a start, he realized that Miss Palmer sat quietly nearby. He was embarrassed to find that he'd completely forgotten her existence while he played. He hadn't acknowledged her once from the moment his fingers touched the keys. Was she annoyed? Most people he knew of her station expected deference. They thought that the world revolved around them.

Her expression gave away nothing as she stood. "I'll get my music." She walked over to a fancy cabinet that had clawed feet. Inside several horizontal shelves created sections and each compartment was filled to the top with what he suspected was sheet music. He snorted softly to himself. Here he'd had to borrow printed music to play at the club and worry about it getting wet or ruined, and she had enough of the stuff to wallpaper the entire room!

She pulled out several music pieces and brought them back to the piano. "I've concentrated on the classics. I don't have any duets."

He shrugged. "I'll add my own little part to it."

"Then let us try this one first."

She had chosen one he didn't know. As she sat down beside him, he caught the whiff of flowers again. "You go ahead, and when you've warmed up a bit, I'll join in," he said.

She started playing and for a while he simply listened, securing in his mind the key she was playing in and getting used to the nuances and emphasis that she placed on certain notes. She played it perfectly, just as it was written. Fifteen bars later, he added a descant, one handed, and then slowly joined in with his other hand.

From that song they went through the next and then the next. Somewhere, about the fourth piece, they switched sides and he played base to her higher notes, she always using the music and he always improvising. He couldn't tell if she was having a good time, but he certainly was enjoying it. The fact that their hands touched a time or two and a pleasant tingle shot up his arm probably had something to do with it.

Her technique, while flawless, was too stiff and formal from his perspective. She would probably make one of his pub tunes sound like a dirge if she ever got around to playing his type of music — which he doubted would ever happen. He nearly laughed out loud at the image — Miss Palmer kicking up her heels, so to speak, with a bawdy pub tune.

"Times up," she said after the sixth piece.

Even though she clearly lacked the ability to improvise and have fun with the music, he'd never come across another pianist who could play so well. She was reserved in style, and strict in a way that left no room for her personality to come through. Unless — he had the disturbing thought — this tightly controlled attitude was her personality. Didn't the music ever move her? He almost asked, but then thought better of it and held his tongue. She would suspect his question only harbored criticism. Besides, he had drawn such pleasure from playing on the Sohmer, he didn't want to sound ungrateful.

Reluctantly, he closed the lid to the keys. "It must be something to play on a piano like this every day."

She rose to her feet and moved back from the instrument, holding herself straight and stiff. "You perform at a pub? Is that right?"

"When I have the time. If there is a rush of customers, then I help my father tend the bar."

"And you never use sheet music?"

He shook his head. "I can read it, but mostly I play by ear."

"So — no formal training?"

"Just what I've figured out along the way." He'd had one old-timer show him how to read music...what the squiggles meant on the lined staff paper, the sharp and flat and natural symbols, and some of the Italian words, but he didn't think that's what she meant by her use of *formal*.

She walked to the door. "I don't think it's going to work out, but I thank you for your time."

"So that's it?"

"Yes. You'll find an envelope on the table in the entryway for you. Compensation for your time."

He rose from the bench. "I thought the idea was to share techniques. We didn't do that."

"I'm afraid that it won't work out after all."

Inside, a spark ignited. Somehow, he felt used. And he didn't like it. He strode over to stand in front of her. From this vantage point, he could see the absolute straightness of the part in her auburn hair and the glossy sheen of its intricate knot. "Why did you really ask me here? And what does your father have to do with it?"

"That doesn't concern you!"

"I'm here, aren't I? So it already does. And I don't like to be made sport of. So tell me."

She pursed her lips. "My father hoped that you could influence my playing for the better."

"We didn't have enough time to figure that out."

She looked away. "Believe me. It was enough."

Meaning his playing lacked in some way. "So what now?"

"Nothing." She shrugged. "You are welcome to go now."

Was that...tears brimming in her eyes? Now he was really curious. He wanted to reach out, to say whatever was going on would work out, but what did he know? He hesitated a moment more, studying her. He didn't want to add to her distress by asking more questions. "All right, Miss Palmer. I'll go. Guess I need to get back to the pub anyway."

He strode down the hall, pausing at the entry table where an envelope with his name lay. He could sure use that money, but taking it would be like getting paid for an hour of pure enjoyment on his part. He might never get to play on such a beautiful instrument again. He couldn't take money for that.

Then again, it was obvious the family had plenty of money and coming here had used up time that he could have been working at the pub. He guessed he'd earned it, although he hated the fact his playing had made Miss Palmer tear up. That soured things some. He grabbed the envelope and stuffed it in his shirt pocket, then walked out the door.

CHAPTER FOUR

It wasn't long after Colin had left that Gloria heard her mother's footsteps in the hallway. They slowed as she stepped into the music room.

"I'll talk about it when Father gets home," Gloria said, before her mother could say anything.

A pause. "All right, dear. I'll...be in the solarium."

She nodded, waited until her mother left, and then sank to the piano bench and stared at the ivory keys.

It was over. All her years of lessons had come to naught. Colin McDougal, with no training and no lessons, had sat down and played circles around her. He had a natural ability, rough as it was, and she obviously didn't. She had thought, with practice, she could learn to play the way people like him did, but the skill had always been elusive, just beyond her grasp. It was that final something — an ability that the great musicians had — a spark in their playing. Mr. McDougal had it and didn't even know it! Hearing him today...she'd never be able to put that kind of emotion into a piece of music. It came from somewhere else inside him all together. It was so bitterly unfair. She'd heard a master pianist — one who was content to play in a pub.

And here she'd thought music was her calling. What a fool she'd been.

When her father came home she would tell him. She would marry George. There was no point in putting him off any longer.

That evening, they didn't discuss it at the table. Mother had always insisted that the help overheard enough as it was, and they mustn't give Clara and Mr. Ross more secrets to banter about in the kitchen. After supper Gloria followed her parents to Father's study.

Father took his seat behind his desk, ready to look through the post that had arrived that day. Mother stood near the fireplace, watching her expectantly.

Gloria shut the door, leaning against it momentarily before turning to face her father. "It's over. Mr. McDougal cannot help me."

Mother clasped her hands together, nearly giddy in her relief. "Then we can move forward with plans for a wedding?"

Gloria should have been braced for the fact that her mother could so easily discard the last eight years of music in her life. After all, Emmeline Palmer did not have a musical bone in her body. Gloria had hoped — obviously foolishly — that her mother would have a bit more empathy for what to Gloria was a life-altering statement.

"I will accept George's offer. That is the sensible thing to do."

"He will be ecstatic that he can move ahead with his plans," Mother said. She walked over to Gloria and hugged her lightly, then pulled back, resting her hands upon Gloria's shoulders. "You'll find that marriage will be a change…but you will grow to like it. You'll be mistress of your own household and entirely too busy to keep up the grueling practice schedule that you have endured of late."

She took Gloria's hand in hers and turned to her husband. "Won't she make a beautiful bride, Stephen? Our little girl…a beautiful young woman now."

Father pulled out his pipe and began filling the bowl with tobacco. "Sit down. The both of you. I want to hear what happened today."

Mother squeezed Gloria's hand reassuringly and then let go to sit in one of the overstuffed leather chairs facing Father. Gloria exhaled, and while the grandfather clock chimed nine times, she took a seat in a chair opposite her father. She explained what had happened that afternoon.

"So you see, Father, we cannot consider him as a tutor. I cannot hope to learn from him. Even he doesn't even know how he plays so brilliantly, which means he certainly cannot teach it to me. I count it ironic of God to have given a tavern player such a gift when he doesn't even recognize it or wish to better himself."

Father drew his brows together. "Are you sure of that? Did you ask him?"

"Well…no. But he seems quite content to work in that pub. He spoke of needing to get back to it more than once."

Father struck a match and held it to the tobacco, drawing and puffing on his pipe to get it started. Then he blew out a cloud of smoke over his head. When he finally spoke, it was slow, deliberate and serious. "You've held onto this dream for a long time, daughter, and now that you are close to realizing it, you have decided to change course?"

This was not what she had expected him to say. She expected him to be relieved that she had finally made up her mind. "Auditioning for the Conservatory was a goal...yes...but I never thought much beyond that—not to the point that I would actually go there to study music."

"Of course not!" Mother broke in. "Girls your age want to marry and have a home of their own. That is the way of the world."

Father studied her a moment before speaking. "So all this preparation, all the piano lessons, have been only for your enjoyment?"

She couldn't admit that she'd always enjoyed the long lessons and practice sessions because she hadn't. There were times she would have preferred to be out on the river, boating with her friends. "I was perfecting a skill."

He blew out a ring of smoke overhead. "Working hard for what I want has put me in the position I am today. It hasn't always been easy, but I never gave up."

"Is that what you think I am doing? Giving up?"

His expression didn't change.

"Well, I'm not! I am simply adjusting my goals. I'm being sensible." She thought that he, as a businessman, would be the first to understand that.

"Your mother has other interests besides music," he finally said. "She has her clubs and social agenda. But I find that nothing gives me more pleasure at the end of a long day than to hear you play."

He stood and walked around the desk. He was an imposing man, tall, wide-shouldered and strong even after all these years away from the ranching he had once known. She could understand how her mother had fallen in love with him so easily. He did tend to get his way. But she couldn't quite understand where he was heading with this line of reasoning.

He stopped in front of her. As if he'd bidden her, she rose to her feet and met his gaze. It was stern and unfathomable, which caused a slight tightening in her gut.

"I'll agree that George would be a suitable man for your husband. He's intelligent, deports himself well, and is financially comfortable. I'll give you no quarrel there."

"He's also handsome," Gloria added.

Father's eyes crinkled into a brief smile. "Yes…I suppose that is important when considering a lifelong companion. I was fortunate your mother was blind regarding that in me."

Father was the most handsome man Gloria had ever known, but then, she might be a bit biased on that account. She opened her mouth to refute him only to realize that he had continued with his thoughts.

"When you do marry you will move away and I will no longer have access to my evening enjoyment.

That may sound selfish to you, but that has something to do with my reasoning here."

"But dear," Mother chided him, leaning forward in her chair. "You cannot expect Gloria to remain with us forever."

He nodded to her, acknowledging her words and then fixed his gaze on Gloria once more. "In all this you have made one misjudgment, daughter. If you will recall on Christmas Eve I asked that, since you were undecided in accepting George's proposal, that you wait until the day of the audition. I find that I must insist upon it now."

"But Father..." She had already made up her mind! George was her best option.

The thunderous frown Father bestowed on her had her closing her mouth tightly.

"It is evident that you wish to please your mother. She, however, is not the one who will live with your choice. You are. I am not ready to let you rush into something unless I believe without a doubt, that it is the best choice for you. I will not be swayed in this."

"Then where does this leave me, Father? The conservatory does not admit married women. I can't have both my dreams—marriage and a position at the conservatory. And George may not wait!"

"As my business associate, I'll make sure he does. The evening of the competition you will choose, but not before then. You may accept Mr. Welbourne's offer of marriage or you can accept your scholarship to the conservatory."

Her eyes teared up. He expected her to place in the top three! She hadn't realized he had such faith in her, misplaced though it was. After hearing Mr. McDougal play, she knew there were others who could play so much better than her. They would be the ones winning the competition. Not her.

"Stephen!" Mother cried out. "This is quite unnecessary. Gloria has already decided."

"Yes, Father. What is the point of waiting?"

He drew his thick brows together. "You are a Palmer. A Palmer does not give up until they've accomplished what they set out to accomplish. I will not settle for less from you. My part in this is that I get five more weeks to enjoy your playing. Your part, is to use this time to figure out what you want most."

He was giving her time? It couldn't be that simple, could it?

Mother looked crestfallen with this turn of events. She probably had been planning the date of the wedding right down to the types of flowers in bloom for the season and the guest list.

"Now," Father continued. "You have five weeks to prepare. What do you intend to do first?"

The line of weeks spread out before her, making her thoughts spin with the possibilities. Not much time to prepare, and yet it was enough to perfect a few more areas of her playing. What should she consider first? "I'm not sure," she said, honestly.

"I'll tell you then. Tomorrow morning you are to persuade this Mr. McDougal to help you whether he wants to or not. If he is as good as you say, then you need to give yourself a chance to study with him. One hour is not enough."

She looked down at her clasped hands. "He said the same thing. I...I didn't want to listen."

"You have come too far to stop now. Sort it out. Put your shoulder into it and get dirty as your Grandmother Mary used to say to me when I was a boy. You have until Valentine's Day."

She was reeling from the turn of the conversation. "Yes, sir." Overwhelmed as she was, the words came out a bit shaky.

He smiled approvingly. "Good. That's what I expect of a Palmer." He hugged her and then opened the door. "Now, off you go. You've got some things to consider before retiring."

She traipsed up the stairs to her room, her mind in turmoil. How was she to face Mr. McDougal after she had already dismissed him? What could she say that would convince him to give her another try?

As Clara helped her out of her bustle and corset and into her soft nightgown, Gloria thought of the next morning and all the scenarios. She could send a note to him and have him meet her here at the house again, but that might have her waiting for several days before he answered. She could go see him. For some reason that held a strange appeal. She seldom had need to travel to the other side of the trolley tracks. She was curious about the place where he played the piano. What type of instrument was he used to using? What sheet music did he have...if any? Catching him off guard when she showed up might be interesting. Perhaps, in that, she would have a certain advantage.

What if he declined to help her? After all, he already had a job at the pub. However, thinking back, his attitude had changed once Mother had offered to pay him for his time. And he had taken the envelope of money quickly enough. He might not turn down a chance to make more.

She climbed into bed and snuggled under the covers. Her past tutor had been stern and at times disagreeable. She wasn't particularly sad to see him leave. But, to work every day with Mr. McDougal...well...he was a very handsome man. Every bit as handsome as George, just in a different way. Blond, wavy hair that swept his collar and deep blue eyes the color of the sea. She recalled the strength and agility in his fingers as they glided over the keys, teasing a delightful counter-melody to her notes. The thought started a low buzz of excitement thrumming inside. She had been aware of his long fingers and of his arm brushing against hers the entire time he had sat beside her on the bench. She shouldn't focus on such things — it was unseemly. But innocent or not, the butterflies in the pit of her stomach refused to settle.

It wouldn't do. He was from a different class and besides that, he could be a bit brash. It was only in the milieu of music that they should communicate. She would persuade him tomorrow. With that, she blew out the candle on the nightstand.

"I'd like to speak with Mr. Colin McDougal, if you please."

Gloria sat alone inside the Palmer coach and practiced the words she would use in just a few moments. Outside, her view of the tree-lined streets gave way to the city park and gazebo along the Potomac River—all looking rather desolate in the wintry gray of the day. The boat house was closed up, and only a few hardy souls, wrapped from head to toe in heavy coats and scarves, fished along the public dock. Still, the sight and scent of the water never failed to lighten her spirit.

Mr. Ross turned the carriage down a cobblestoned street a few blocks from the water where the shops and businesses stood close together like tall sentinels of shades of greens and browns and tan. Burgundy awnings flapped and billowed in the breeze and cast shadows on the clumps of snow that littered the sidewalk. The sound of the horses' hooves striking the stones slowed and then slowed further. *Adaggio.* For heaven's sake! She was thinking in musical terms! She must be nervous.

The carriage stopped before a two-story building with dark green shutters on the windows and a matching dark green door. Mr. Ross climbed from his driver's seat and positioned the movable step for her. He offered his hand to help her alight from the carriage. She held her bonnet secure with one hand as she stared up at the sign overhead, painted in gold and burgundy red paint, announcing McDougal's Pub.

"You should wait here, Miss Palmer. I'll see if Mr. McDougal is in," Mr. Ross said.

"Thank you."

He entered and spoke to a burley man behind the bar. The reflection on the windowpanes made it difficult for her to see inside very well. The place looked empty of customers. She inched closer, curious about the piano Mr. McDougal played on here.

"Help you, Miss?"

A dark-haired young man near her age tipped his cap to her. He carried a wooden rack filled with dirty empty jars.

"Can I help you?" he said again. "This here is my place."

"I'm waiting for Mr. McDougal. Mr. Colin McDougal. My driver just entered to make inquiries."

"You're welcome inside. The place is empty except for my family." He opened the door for her.

"No. No, I couldn't. I'll wait here." Through the open doorway, she spied a pair of legs clad in men's gray trousers extending from behind a battered upright piano. The man rose up to his knees and reached around to the front of the piano, pushing down on one of the keys several times before disappearing behind the instrument once more. It was Mr. McDougal.

"Hey, Colin!" the young boy called out. "There's a lady here asking for you."

"Be a minute. Almost got this fixed." His answer returned muffled.

The young man stepped inside all the way and nudged Mr. McDougal's boot with his foot. "It's not Tamara."

Not Tamara? Gloria stopped the door before it shut. Curious now, she stepped all the way inside. The scent of onions and stew meat came to her, incongruent with the way she had expected a pub to smell. Didn't taverns smell of liquor and sweat and unwashed bodies?

Footsteps and then a sudden loud thump sounded overhead. "We're fine, Shaun!" a woman called out, her voice coming from a steep stairwell at the back of the room. "A pot just got away from me."

Mr. Ross, in earnest conversation with the bartender, stopped talking mid-sentence when he saw Gloria. "Miss Palmer!"

"I will speak with Mr. McDougal myself," she said. It was bold of her to come into such a place, but with another woman here, and with the place obviously empty of customers, she felt a bit safer in doing so.

The piano had to be at least twenty-five years old. Despite a patina of lemon oil, numerous scratches in the darkly-stained wood revealed a rough life for the instrument. Three ivory keys were cracked and looked like they'd been glued back together. One key was missing altogether.

"Give me an E-flat, up a couple of octaves, James. Then go right up the scale," Colin called out, his voice muffled.

James snorted. "Like I remember what notes those are."

"You're not much help. Second key of a pair of the black keys."

James reached for the keyboard an octave too low. Seeing that, Gloria leaned down and played the correct note, and then ran her fingers up the scale.

"That's it. You got it," Colin said. "One more time. I just have to tighten this wire…"

Gloria played the C-minor chord.

Colin froze at the sound of the more complex chord. Then he scrambled from behind the piano, his blond hair tousled and his face ruddy with exertion. When he recognized her, the open expression quickly evaporated, leaving a slight frown in its place. "Miss Palmer. What are you doing here?"

She offered a small, hopefully brave, smile, suddenly unsure of the wisdom of coming to see him here. Maybe it was the size of the room, but he suddenly looked bigger than he had in her house. Both he and the young man towered over her by eight inches or more. Mr. McDougal's coarse cotton shirt strained over his broad shoulders, and the brown suspenders he wore emphasized the muscles beneath. He had rolled his sleeves up to his elbows, and now wiped his hands on a red rag as he waited for her to speak. If they had been back in her music room, she would feel much more confident in persuading him to see things her way. Now…she wasn't so sure. This was his home. By coming here, she may have given up her advantage after all. "I'd like a word with you, Mr. McDougal."

Colin glanced over and noted Mr. Ross at the bar watching both of them. "It's Colin here."

She was uncomfortable using his given name when she barely knew him, but she wanted things to be easy between them. If he agreed to help her, they'd be spending a lot of time together. "Colin, then."

"That's my da behind the bar. Shaun McDougal." He called over to his father. "Da? This is Miss Palmer, the woman I spoke about."

"Welcome to McDougal's, Miss Palmer," the beefy man said. "And pleased to meet you."

She nodded politely.

"Can I get you a glass of water?" Colin asked.

"No, thank you." Then she realized he looked warm, even though the room was quite cool. A bead of perspiration trickled down his temple. He could probably use one. "But you go ahead and get one for yourself if you'd like. I can wait." She wanted him as comfortable as possible...so that his answer to her would be 'yes.' She wasn't sure what she would do if he said no. Send her father to persuade him? That didn't sound conducive to a good working relationship.

Colin shook his head—just the slightest movement, his manner reserved.

Perhaps she hadn't been the most gracious of hostesses yesterday.

"I see you met, James, my brother."

She looked aside at the younger Mr. McDougal. "Yes. He was kind enough to invite me inside when he saw me on the street."

James grinned. "I knew who you were. Colin mentioned a few things when he came home yesterday."

Gloria wasn't sure what to make of that. What had he said about her? Likely nothing too complimentary.

Colin spun his rag into a twisted rope and snapped it softly at his brother's thigh. "Get moving. Those need washing."

Flashing a quick smirk, James grabbed the rack of dirty jars and carried them to the back room.

Colin turned back and met her gaze. "Now what's this all about?"

She couldn't just blurt it out. She glanced at the row of empty tables. "May we sit?"

He nodded and pulled out a nearby chair for her, then sat down opposite her. He looked so comfortable, his shoulders relaxed, his hair tousled with a longish piece sweeping down and almost covering one eye. She had noticed his eyes yesterday. Now she wondered at his age. Older than she, but not by too much. And tall and lean, like he still had some filling out to do before he was finished growing. He was handsome and likely had someone he was sweet on. Tamara, perhaps? It hardly mattered one way or the other. She was interested in him as a piano teacher. Nothing more. She pulled her thoughts back to the task before her.

"Are you familiar with the Marlowe Conservatory?"

"It'd be hard not to know of it since it's right here in town."

There was an edge to his voice that she didn't understand. "But you know what it is?"

"A music school." He raised his chin. "Not that they would let someone like me inside."

"I'm not sure I understand you."

He blew out a breath before answering. "Someone without the means to pay. Not everyone is born with a silver spoon."

What did he expect her to say to that? She certainly had no knowledge of the conservatory's rules.

When she didn't comment, he looked over his shoulder at Mr. Ross, who had settled on a stool at the bar. Then Colin clasped his hands together on the table as he leaned forward and cocked his head. "So tell me. What has the conservatory got to do with me?"

She took a deep breath. "The entry auditions take place in five weeks. On Valentine's Day. And I want you to help me prepare for them."

"That's not what you said yesterday. Yesterday you said I wasn't good enough." The accusation hung in the air between them.

That's what he thought? She hadn't realized that she left him with that impression. It was completely wrong. *She* was the one lacking, not him. Again, she was struck by the thought that he didn't realize the talent he possessed.

"I've had a chance to think more about it and I've reconsidered. You *will* be able to help me."

She wouldn't allow anything else. For that matter, neither would her father, considering he'd forced this waiting period on her and wanted her to make good use of it. She *was* a Palmer and his blood coursed through her. She would show him. If necessary, she would practice until her fingers bled. Perhaps he would be happy with her then.

"Can't your father pay your way in?"

"Contrary to what you have been led to believe, it doesn't work that way. Admittance is based on merit, not financial means."

He shook his head. "I don't believe that. Most people in this world don't turn away good money."

"Suffice it to say that I want to earn my way. I…don't want to take another's place simply because my family can afford the tuition."

His gaze narrowed on her.

She held still. She would not let him see her squirm.

The way he studied her was rather unsettling. It was as though he could see more than she wanted him to see. "It isn't about the money," he said slowly. "You need the validation."

She stiffened. "I don't need the validation. I don't need anything," she said defensively.

"Right," he said flatly.

"I cannot help it if you don't believe me."

He blew out a long breath. "What's in it for me?"

She frowned. She wasn't used to being addressed in such a way or, for that matter, talking about money. It was…inappropriate for a woman of her station to concern herself with such things. "You'll be well paid for your time. Just like yesterday."

His gaze never left hers. "Fair enough. What changed between yesterday and today?"

"Nothing changed but my mind."

"There's more to it than that. If I'm going to do this, you have to be honest with me."

She closed her eyes and inhaled through her nose, drawing on her own strength. When she opened them, she focused on her gloved hands. "My father reminded me—quite vehemently—that a Palmer doesn't give up. Ever. He also reminded me that I have five weeks and I had better use every one of them."

"So it is about his pride? Family pride?"

She hated to think of it like that, however by all appearances, it looked to be the case. She nodded. "I believe so."

He sat back. "All right then. I know something about that."

She breathed a little easier. Had they reached common ground?

"What happens if you don't win? What then?"

The animosity in his eyes had lessened, replaced by something else…curiosity? "Then I will accept George Welbourne's offer of marriage. We are practically engaged now as it is. I only need to satisfy my father's wishes to wait until after the audition to give him my answer."

He didn't reply for the longest time, and then suddenly he drummed his fingers on the marred tabletop. "How many hours are we talking about?"

Hope started to buzz in her chest. Up until that moment, she had expected him to decline her offer, but he was actually considering it! "As many as you can afford."

"Until the audition on February 14th and then what happens…happens." He rubbed his chin, the motion drawing her attention to the fine stubble that peppered his jaw. "It would mean rearranging things here at the pub. Most days I'll need to be back here by four."

"I'm willing to start early…as early as you wish. And I'll make sure to be warmed up by the time you arrive."

The corner of his mouth raised slightly.

Likely she was beginning to sound desperate which was not the best position in a negotiation.

However, he wanted honesty and she was honestly desperate. Oh, why didn't he give her a definite answer?

"Can I call you Gloria?" he asked slyly.

Was this his way? To constantly push the boundaries of propriety? Had she made a mistake in trusting him? Yet for her, it was in for a penny, in for a pound. Ignoring the small voice inside that asked what her mother would think — or George — she swallowed and then nodded. How she would explain her familiarity with a tutor, she'd figure out later.

He grinned then and stood, grabbing his red rag from the table and stuffing it in his hip pocket. "I have to get to work."

"But you haven't given me your answer!" She stood, her hands braced on the tabletop.

"I will. Tomorrow. I need to talk it over with my family. If I am gone, things will change around here They will have to pick up the slack, so they should be in on the decision."

She hadn't expected his choice to involve more than the two of them. Would his family sway him against her? Much less sure of herself now, she asked, "What time can I expect you?"

"I'll let you know tomorrow morning."

She had to pin him down more than that. "Nine o'clock?"

He nodded, studying her again in that way of his.

"Very well. I will be prepared to work, just in case the answer is yes."

"Good day to you, Gloria."

The twinkle in his blue eyes held her captive. She found herself intrigued...and barely breathing. "Good day...Colin."

He slipped on his cap and turned toward the back room, whistling a tune that sounded decidedly Irish.

CHAPTER FIVE

Colin snugged up his collar as he tromped through the two inches of new snow that had fallen during the night. The ice on the river was thick enough now to cut and haul back to the warehouse. When would he fit the time in to do that if he was busy giving music lessons?

This entire music lesson thing seemed far-fetched. How had Miss Palmer come up with his name? That chance meeting at the dinner club? He had his doubts that he could help her. Heck, he had his doubts that she really wanted his help. It sounded like her father was the one pushing her. Except...she had gone out of her way to come to the pub and ask him. He couldn't figure it out—not yet anyway. And it mattered very little in the long run. He'd do his part and then walk away with a nice chunk of money.

His family—meaning Da—had reluctantly agreed to his change of work schedule as long as Colin was there every evening to help when the pub was busiest. With Patrick, and now Colin gone, Da would have to work harder to keep things running smoothly. James crowed about having more responsibility which didn't surprise Colin. The way that Colin felt about his music was the way James felt about the pub. After that discussion, Colin had gone to bed and wrestled with his conscience throughout the night.

He could sure use the money. And like the night he got paid for playing in the club, he would be doing the thing he loved. He'd make sure to put half of his pay in the family jar. After all...they were giving him this opportunity. Maybe, if things went well, he'd be able to buy a new piano for the pub. The one they had was fifty years old and in constant need of tuning. Wouldn't Tamara be shocked to see him walk right into the music shop on Ninth Street and order a new one?

Miss Palmer...Gloria...had surprised him. At her home, he quickly realized that her mother ran the house and Gloria acquiesced to her leadership. She was anxious to please her mother and now, it seemed she was anxious to please her father. Did she ever do something to please herself?

Never, in a million years had he expected to see her walk into McDougal's. He hadn't thought she had it in her! Granted, it had been morning and no customers had been inside, but all in all it was not a usual place for a woman of her class. Maybe there was more to her than he'd given her credit for. Maybe she had enough gumption to actually pull off her scheme.

It tugged at him—the one answer that she'd given when he asked her what would happen if she failed to win the audition. 'I'll forget this dream of mine and marry Welbourne.' She said it so matter-of-fact. Like…I had porridge for breakfast or the sky is blue. And there, he realized, was the rub. Because if she truly wanted to marry this fellow, wouldn't she just do it? And yet she was going along with her father's edict. Just what kind of a family were the Palmers? Did being rich mean a young woman couldn't marry whoever she wanted? That she had to marry for position? For security?

Why should he care? Because for some reason…he did. Her anxious face had haunted his dreams. She had tried to cover up the worry, but she hadn't succeeded. Even though it wasn't any of his business, he did want to help her.

He turned down the cobblestone street that led to her house—the last one at the end. It backed up to the Potomac River. A dock and boathouse sat on their property, along with a carriage house large enough to house the horses and the coach that he'd seen her climb into yesterday after leaving the pub. Large trees, naked of leaves this time of year, lined the river and sectioned off the property from the other houses on the street.

When he stepped up onto the wide veranda, Mr. Ross opened the door and ushered him in, taking his hat and coat. "Follow me." The sound of piano scales echoed down the long hall.

When he and Mr. Ross stepped into the room, Gloria stopped playing. "Thank you," she said, dismissing her butler. Then she rose from the piano bench and addressed him. "I'm so glad that you came!"

"I said I would."

She wore a pale, ice pink gown with lace at her collar and at the ends of her sleeves. Her dark auburn hair was piled high on top of her head, with three corkscrew curls sweeping over her shoulder on the left. He'd never seen anyone more beautiful — or at the moment — more unsure by the expression on her face. "Have you come to a decision?"

"I have questions."

She turned up one palm. "Then ask away."

"I'm not sure why you want me instead of hiring someone that has experience in tutoring. It doesn't make sense."

"I alerted Mr. Sharrell at the music store regarding my need for a tutor. No one has come forward. I suppose for such a short time as five weeks, no one wanted to upend their life."

"Guess I can understand that."

"So, you will do it?" she asked worriedly.

His heart skipped a beat at the hope on her face. She didn't seem like other rich people he'd run up against over the years. She seemed...nice. "I'm willing."

She exhaled a shaky breath. "Wonderful. Then let's get busy. I'm all warmed up. Do you have an idea where we should start?"

"We should start with the audition. I want to know more about what will be expected of you. Have you ever auditioned before? Have they sent instructions?"

"Good point." She walked over to the music cabinet and withdrew a large folder of papers from the top segment. "I have it here. And no...I've never auditioned before."

He followed her and read over the requirements the Marlowe Conservatory had outlined. Gloria would have to play two songs — a classic and one of her choice. He read further down. The auditions were open to anyone over the age of sixteen. There were a total of ten spots. Only the musicians who placed in the top three spots would be invited to study at the conservatory. He read that twice. Competition would be stiff. He hadn't expected any less.

Gloria bumped gently against his arm. Through his sleeve, his skin tingled. Did she even notice how close she stood? She seemed to be engrossed in reading the page he held. The sweet scent of roses drifted up and enveloped him. He swallowed and tried to concentrate on the audition rules. "It says one piece should be classical. Do you have something in mind or should we go through a few and see first how you play them?"

She pulled out the music for three classical pieces. "Are you familiar with any of these?"

He studied the notes on the page while at the same time hearing the notes in his head. The pages fluttered as her hand trembled. He hadn't realized that he'd leaned in so close. He was near enough to see her pulse throbbing at the base of her throat. Near enough to touch her there and feel the smooth softness of her skin. He glanced up.

She stared at him, her green eyes wide and innocent.

Heat suffused his face. He pulled back, mumbling, "Excuse me." He had best watch himself or he'd be let go before he's even finished one lesson.

A woman like her, of her quality, wouldn't think twice about dallying with someone like him. And a man like Mr. Palmer wouldn't think twice about firing him. He wanted this job. And darn if he didn't want to see her have her moment of glory in that audition.

He blew out a breath and pointed to first one title on the sheet music and then another. "I've heard these two before. Not the other."

"Have you played them?

"No."

She walked with them to the piano, sat down on the bench, and arranged the sheet music on the stand.

"Go ahead." He took the chair at her side and prepared to turn the pages as she needed.

She played the first one, *Piano Sonata in A Minor* by Schubert, and then with only a minute to readjust, moved right into the second one, *Concerto No.3 in D Major* by Bach.

He found himself mesmerized by the flight of her fingers on the keys, and the graceful bend of her wrists as she played. No rings sparkled or gleamed on her fingers. Clean hands. Clean nails. He glanced down at this own hands and found them scarred from his work at the pub and stained with dried ink from his scribblings of songs.

As she played, he began to sense something he couldn't quite put a name to. The first piece was moody and flowing, and she had played it perfectly as far as he could tell. The second piece was technically more challenging, and she slowed down at three of the more difficult areas. She followed the notes and the italicized instructions of *adagio, legato,* and *fortissimo,* and a few he had no idea of what they meant. Again, he wondered how he would be able to help her when she had had so much more instruction than he and knew so much more than he did. Her years of lessons trumped his years of dabbling at the keys.

"One more," he said when she had finished Bach's piece. "Do you need a break before moving on to the last one?"

She stretched out her fingers and then clenched her hands. "What did you think so far?"

"You played perfectly except for the areas where you slowed down due to the difficulty."

"You caught that?" She inclined her head.

Of course, he'd caught it. "Are you surprised?"

"No. Oh no," she said quickly, backtracking. "Rather, I'm pleased that you noticed. That you are aware…that you noticed small details… It is a good thing." Her face reddened as she stumbled over her thoughts. "I only hoped I could play it well enough that you wouldn't notice those slower parts at all." She let out a soft laugh. "Apparently not."

"If you choose a different piece of music for the competition, no one will know."

"I'll know." Her smile grew. "And now you will too."

She looked vulnerable, sweet. Nothing like the woman he had first met. That woman had been ramrod stiff, her words clipped and short. Suddenly he realized that he had answered her with a grin of his own.

In that moment, something passed between them. An understanding. A coming together.

Suddenly seeming to recognize the fact, Gloria turned back to the piano and arranged the sheet music on the stand so that the third piece was displayed. "We should move on."

Next, she played a tune that he enjoyed by a man named Mendelssohn. It was lighter than the other two.

"My guess is you should work on the one by Bach. If you can master that one, you'll be ahead of any other contenders. And it is the least boring of the three."

She smiled slightly. "I was afraid you might say that. I have my work cut out for me then."

"With practice, you'll be able to get through it just fine." He thought it must be nice to spend all day at the piano. He'd never gotten that chance. Work and chores had always come first.

"I know this one doesn't have the same...zip?...as the songs you are used to. I hope, over the next weeks, that I won't bore you to tears with playing it until it is perfect." She shuffled the music into a pile and took it back to the cabinet. "All right. Now for the second piece — the one that is not classical."

He wasn't ready to move on. "What happened with your last music teacher?"

"Mr. Peers?" She hesitated slightly before answering. "Father let him go."

"Wasn't he doing his job?"

She sighed. "Yes. But once I asked about auditioning for the conservatory, he changed. He tried to discourage me from auditioning. He said that I needed another year of practice, perhaps even two, before I would be ready. I became suspicious. After all, he'd been my tutor for three years."

"I'd think that he'd encourage you to try out. Even if you didn't win, it would be good preparation for the following year."

"You'd think that, wouldn't you? Just before Christmas, I learned that Mr. Peers's son, Joseph, was also planning to audition. Father fired Mr. Peers immediately, saying it was a conflict of interest." She blew out a breath. "So there I was, without a tutor."

"And then you saw me at the club…"

"When I heard you play…" she hesitated again slightly, "…I was enthralled. I thought perhaps God had thrown me a lifeline."

He snorted softly. No one had ever thought of him like that before. "Or a bone."

She laughed suddenly and her green eyes sparkled with mischief. "You are no bone, Mr. McDougal. Although my…fascination with your playing may have been because Mr. Welbourne proposed at that exact same instant."

"So I ruined the moment for him?" Could be that was a good thing.

"Is that a smirk, Mr. McDougal?"

"If you had answered him right off, I have the feeling that I wouldn't have a job here now."

"True."

She was prettier when she was relaxed. "I'd like to see you get accepted into Marlowe's. I am looking forward to the challenge. And I thought we agreed on Colin."

"Yes. Colin." She sighed. "I'm hungry. Are you?"

His smile grew into a grin.

A shadow fell across the floor as Mrs. Palmer opened the door wider. "I haven't heard any music for a while. What is going on?"

Beside him, Gloria stiffened. "Mother! We were just discussing which music to consider for the second piece."

He rose to his feet.

The tension in the room escalated at least ten degrees as the older woman's gaze pinned him. "And have you decided?"

"Not yet," he said. What had happened with this woman? Why the change from last week when he had first met her? She had been pleasant before...cordial and welcoming. He wasn't sensing that anymore.

Gloria took a short step forward. "We thought we'd continue the discussion over luncheon."

Mrs. Palmer turned back to Gloria. "I'll tell Mary to set another place."

"Thank you, Mother. We'll be right along."

"See that you are," she said, her tone clipped, before she left the room.

Colin raised his brows. "I think she'd like me to leave."

Gloria shook her head. "Please don't take it personally. This...edict of Father's upset her. It disrupted her carefully planned life, which means she isn't arranging my wedding right now. She will be fine when the audition is over."

For some reason, he didn't like being reminded of her plans after the audition. With her musical ability, she could go far with her playing. "Can you give music up so easily after the audition?" he asked.

"Mother says being able to play the piano is the mark of an accomplished woman. The entire point is to bring an air of peace and culture to the home."

"And that's enough for you? You are willing to give up the conservatory to marry?"

Her lashes fluttered down. "I haven't secured a place there yet and I'm hardly a performer."

He couldn't believe what he was hearing. And then he realized what was going on. She was being pulled in two directions and trying to please both of her parents. "The audition was your father's idea."

Her brows drew together in a troubled expression. "Father is the one who mentioned your name when Mr. Peers left. He remembered your performance—or rather—he remembered my fascination with your performance."

And here he'd thought it was his playing at the club that had prompted *her* to request him as a tutor. Apparently, he was wrong. Guess it was a bit of ego on his part that he had wished that were the case. "So, that's the whole of it," he said, seeing the situation clearly now. "The audition is the goal. Win or lose."

"Yes."

But her troubled expression remained. She wasn't sure. He could see that plain as day. Maybe, just maybe, the audition did mean more to her than she realized.

"How did things go today?" Father asked as they finished their evening meal.

Although she was buzzing with excitement on the inside, she realized that Mother was sorely disappointed in the recent turn of events. She had hoped to be planning a wedding at this point. Her attitude had put a damper on the entire meal. "We decided on the classical piece — the one by Bach."

"Isn't that different than what Mr. Peers had planned for you?"

It surprised her that Father knew what she had been practicing. She hadn't realized that he'd paid such close attention. "Yes. Colin — I mean Mr. McDougal" — she corrected herself quickly — "feels that will show off the widest range of my ability."

"And you agree with him?"

"Yes," she said simply. "Perhaps you were right about Mr. Peers. He wasn't looking to my best interests."

Father set down his linen napkin and stood. He moved to her mother's place and pulled out her chair for her. "Fine dinner, dear."

"A word with you, Stephen? In the study?"

Gloria took that to mean that *she* would be the object of discussion. Whenever Mother was distressed over something, she would request a private moment with Father. Mother wouldn't try to sway him into foregoing the audition, would she? Gloria had enjoyed today — enjoyed discussing music with Colin. It was much different than her lessons had been with Mr. Peers. Colin treated her as an equal when it came to music. She'd never had that before. She would hate to lose the opportunity to work with him now that they had started.

It had been a long day — a productive day. And she wanted nothing to put a damper on her sense of accomplishment. Colin had agreed to come two days a week to work with her and said they could negotiate later if she thought she needed him more toward the end.

Mr. Ross helped her with her chair. She thanked him, stopped in the kitchen to thank Mary for the meal, and then climbed the stairs to her bedroom, humming the music she'd played all day. It kept running through her head, along with thoughts of Colin. He liked to pace as he listened. That was different than Mr. Peers who liked to hover over her like a vulture and watch her fingers on the keys. Once, when Colin had come near to turn the page for her, she had caught the lingering scent of soap from his morning wash. It was strange. In that moment, the skin on her neck had gone from cold to hot to cold again. She'd fumbled with the notes and had to start the refrain again.

Two days…two long days before he came back.

She opened her hope chest and withdrew the quilt she had been working on. With the batting and back now slip-stitched in place, it was time to begin the intricate hand-stitches to secure it all. She sat in the rocker by the glowing hearth, humming as she worked, at first thinking of Grandmother Mary and the love she'd poured into making the pink flower basket design on the front. She had been young, her hair still in braids, as she listened to her

Grandmother pray over the quilt, asking for a good and godly man, to be Gloria's husband.

Gloria had piped up and said she just wanted a man that could play and make her laugh like her brother Tad.

Grandma had just smiled and said, *Perhaps you'll get both.*

Gloria lowered her needle and material to her lap. Her thoughts lingering on her brother.

Tad was usually on her side…when a side had to be chosen. His opinion had always mattered to her. He was much like Father — smart and quick-witted. She remembered the way he had railed against Mother and Father's rules, angry at them for pushing him to follow in Father's footsteps when all he wanted was to make his own way in the world. When she was twelve, he'd been nineteen and finally had enough of the tug and pull. He left home. At the time, he had said he was sorry most of all, for leaving her.

Tad, she realized suddenly, was a lot like Colin. She would love to know what he thought of her new tutor and if they would get on well with each other. Oh, how she wished he were here now.

The thought brought her full circle to George. She had never considered what Tad would think of George.

How odd.

CHAPTER SIX

Saturday dawned clear and crisp, the sun shining down but offering little warmth. In the shed behind the pub, Colin moved aside the bags of sawdust that Da had stored there earlier in the fall, making room for the ice that would be stored there. The physical labor was not strenuous enough to keep his mind occupied, and as he had discovered lately, his thoughts circled around to Gloria and her coming audition.

It was already the nineteenth of January. The month was half over, which drew the day of Gloria's audition ever closer. He counted out the number of practice sessions that they had left. Seven…twice a week…the last one on the twelfth of February.

The creaking of heavy wood and iron wheels signaled James's return from the livery with a mule and a wagon. He held the mule steady in the alleyway while Colin loaded the tools he would need to section out the ice onto the flatbed—pick axes, a shovel, a saw, a spike and hammer, ice tongs and extra old blankets.

"What about the skates?" James asked. "Just one race."

"One race," Colin agreed. He loaded their ice skates. A race across the ice with his brother would get his blood pumping.

Did Gloria skate? The random thought would have caught him off guard if he hadn't thought about her constantly from the start of their practice sessions. It wore on him now. He knew his chances at anything other than a professional relationship with her were nil and yet he enjoyed spending time with her. According to people in her world, he was on the wrong side of the tracks. She might need him now for lessons. But the minute February 14th came and the auditions were over, he would no longer matter to her.

He climbed up to sit beside James. His brother flicked the reins and they started for the river.

"I'm glad you could do this today," James said. "Da is slowing down."

Colin nodded. He'd noticed.

They headed toward a shallow area, a quarter-of-a-mile south of the public pier, where they harvested ice every year. Colin liked the ice to be six inches thick to make it worth his sweat and labor. Six to eight inches assured him the ice would last into the summer before melting completely away. Twelve inches was even better, but then the ice became too heavy and unwieldy. James stopped the mule and Colin jumped down. Together, working with the mule, they angled the wagon back to the edge of the frozen water.

James jumped down and staked the mule's tie line, then grabbed his skates. "Race first, work later."

Colin hesitated. He could hear Da's voice in his head saying the opposite. *Work first, then fun.*

"Come on," James urged. "If we load up the ice first, we'll be too tired to have a proper race. And I aim to beat you this time."

Colin grabbed his skates and sat down on the edge of the flatbed to put them on. He scanned the ice and the box elder trees along the bank, then pointed with his chin. "Silver maple and back?"

James grinned. "This is my year."

Colin cuffed him on the head. "It's only that as long as Patrick isn't here. He beats the both of us."

"Think he'll be back after that row with Da?"

"Yeah, he'll be back. When it comes down to it, he's family. He and Da need to cool off a bit."

They walked down to the river and, the moment their blades touched the ice, took off.

It didn't take Colin long to realize his brother had gotten stronger and faster over the past year. He stretched as tall as Colin now and pushed off hard with each long leg. Colin had to work harder than ever before to keep abreast of him.

At the maple, they slid to a scraping stop and then headed back to the starting point. Colin breathed deep and hard, his heart pounding in his chest with each strong push of his feet. They raced against the wind now and the cold air froze his cheeks and nose and made his eyes tear up. Beside him, James pushed ahead. Colin gave one final effort and raced in front of his brother to win.

They leaned over, hands on their thighs, winded.

"One more time?" James said.

Colin shook his head. "Today, I'm walking away the winner."

James grinned. "Your days are numbered."

Colin was sure they were. James still had some growing to do, and next year he'd have the edge with his longer legs. Colin straightened, clapping him on the shoulder. "Come on. Let's get this done."

Cutting out the blocks of ice took the better part of the day. While they worked, they could hear shouts and laughter coming from the park upriver. Just before noon, Ma showed up with warm apple cider and hearty sandwiches, which they devoured in a matter of seconds. Wrapped up as he was in getting the job done, Colin ignored the people strolling by on the path that skirted the river. By early afternoon he and his brother were hot and sweaty despite the cold, and loading the last of the blocks onto the wagon.

Two couples, strolling abreast and conversing, approached along the walking path. Colin paid them no mind at first, but then he recognized Gloria's voice. He stopped mid-step, the last block of ice hefted up on one shoulder as he made his way up the bank to the flatbed. Her cheeks were pink from the bite of the wind and her eyes sparkled from beneath a burgundy felt hat as she laughed at something the woman walking ahead of her said. He couldn't help but notice that the fit of her matching burgundy woolen coat complemented her trim figure. Her hands were stuffed into a white rabbit-fur muff. She hadn't noticed him.

On her one side, his arm looped with hers, walked the man he'd seen on the first night at Tarkington's. His overcoat and gloves looked to be of the finest quality. Probably straight out of New York City. A top hat crowned him and he wore a dark gold silk scarf at his neck. In his free hand, he held two pair of ice skates, the blades gleaming new and sharp.

So this was Welbourne — the man who had asked for her hand in marriage. Colin felt the sting of comparison, even though he knew they were all the same in the Lord's eyes. He couldn't help it. He'd never felt more aware of the differences between them...he and James laboring away in their work clothes and thick boots, while Gloria and the man appeared perfectly collected and beautiful. Anonymity might be the best way to handle the situation, considering how unkempt and sweaty he was at the moment.

In that second of hesitation, he realized that any connection he might feel with her had only to do with the music between them. She had her rich boyfriend. Her rich life. He was a fool to think he'd felt any spark of an actual friendship there. He hoped she would walk on by without noticing him. He wasn't ashamed of his lot. He provided an honest service to his family, but he didn't want her to see him. Not here. Not now.

"Miss Palmer!" James hailed her, jumping down from the wagon.

Great. Leave it to his brother.

Gloria stopped walking. "Why…hello, Master McDougal." Her gaze darted to Colin, and recognition filled her eyes. "Colin!"

He finished his walk to the wagon and hefted the block of ice onto the flatbed. "Miss Palmer," he said with a small nod. He'd been surprised that she called him by his given name in front of her friends. Surprised and pleased.

"*This* is him?" The woman on Gloria's other side spoke behind her gloved hand. The woman, along with the other two men, looked Colin over from his shoes to his head.

Colin squashed the urge to run his fingers through his hair. It could probably use smoothing down, but he wouldn't give them the satisfaction of revealing his discomfort at their perusal.

"Surprising, isn't it?" Welbourne said.

Colin glanced at James. They'd both encountered snobbery before, but with keeping to the pub and the beer runs for the most part, James seldom ran up against it. For all that, James recognized it now. His brother's face had become stone.

Colin grabbed his rag from his back pocket and wiped the sweat that dripped into his eyes. Then he raised his chin. "I didn't catch your names," he said, challenging them to speak directly to him, but keeping his focus on Welbourne.

The woman let out a small indignant gasp.

"Why would you?" Welbourne said, lifting his chin, his eyes mere slits.

Meaning they didn't intend to give their names. Colin didn't have time for this. And he didn't like that Gloria walked with them—any of them, but especially the man she was arm-in-arm with. Colin turned back to the wagon and threw the tarp over the top of the ice.

"Her name is Elizabeth."

Gloria's soft voice sliced through the haze of resentment that encased him. He turned back to face her. She had extricated herself from Welbourne's arm.

"Elizabeth and John Huntley," she continued, "I'd like you to meet Colin McDougal, my music tutor, and his younger brother James."

On the opposite side of the wagon, his brother waited to cinch down the tarp, holding his rope against his thigh.

Colin stood his ground, his jaw tight. It wasn't Gloria he was angry with.

"Mr. McDougal, this is George Welbourne."

"The third," Welbourne added with a smirk. "I wouldn't have expected cutting ice to be such dirty work.

Colin couldn't bring himself to nod, bow, or in any way acknowledge the man. He didn't like him. And even though it wasn't any of his business, he sure didn't like the idea that Gloria planned to marry him.

"Come, dear..." Welbourne said, taking Gloria's arm again.

Gloria did not move.

"We are heading to the rink at the park."

Was she simply making a statement? Or was it a poor invitation?

Welbourne scowled. "Come now, Gloria. Leave the man to his work. Isn't it enough that he monopolizes your time at the piano? I deserve to have you to myself for the afternoon."

Gloria pressed her lips together.

Colin didn't particularly want to join them either. Da would be expecting him and James back at the pub as it was. He leveled his gaze at Welbourne. "Another time."

Welbourne snorted. "Right. Another time."

The urge to put Welbourne in his place in a much more physical manner came in ever-increasing waves. With the few words the man had uttered, Colin realized where he'd heard him before. He was the man that had tried to buy the pub in the summer. Because of Welbourne, Da had had the row with Patrick which had severed the family.

"We could take him," James said under his breath. "Your move."

It was tempting. *A little help here, Lord. You know that turning my other cheek has never been a talent.*

It was almost as if Gloria could sense his aggressive thoughts, she watched him so closely. Colin clamped his teeth together and then shook his head tightly to answer his brother. He wouldn't embarrass her with a public brawl.

"Have a good day, Miss Palmer," he said, ignoring the smirk on Welbourne's face. "I'll see you on Tuesday."

"Come on," Welbourne said and turned Gloria back toward the path.

"Was that necessary, George?" she asked as they walked away.

Colin watched a minute, and then he motioned to James to toss the end of the rope to him. It sailed over the wagon and he caught the end of it, pulling it tightly to cinch it down over the tarp, while James did likewise on the opposite side.

"We're ready," Colin said as he stored the skates and the tools they'd used beneath the wagon seat. "Get the mule."

James untied the mule and then climbed up onto the wagon seat.

"Did you recognize him?" Colin asked, his gaze following the small group that strolled along the river walk. They were out of hearing distance now.

His brother nodded. "A race would have been even better. Between you and me, we could beat that dandified peacock and his friend there."

Colin relaxed slightly. Leave it to James to make things interesting. "We could at that."

He climbed up onto the bench seat and took the reins from his brother, then gave a sharp, whistle and flicked the reins, urging the mule to get moving.

CHAPTER SEVEN

Gloria looked longingly at the rich-brown leather satchel in the window-case of Sharrell's Music Emporium. It would be perfect for Colin to store his papers in, but she knew he would never accept it. The satchel was a bit over the top as an apology for what had happened at the river on Saturday.

She stepped into the store, enjoying the familiar light tinkling of bells overhead. The emporium had three new grand pianos and two more that were the smaller, against-the-wall, type. Those reminded her of Colin's — the one at the pub.

A young woman stood behind the counter. "May I help you, Miss? Is there something particular you are looking for?"

A twenty-five-cent piece of atonement? she considered saying, but then knew that would only sound odd to the woman. "Is Mr. Sharrell here?"

"He's out for the morning, Miss. My name is Tamara Harding."

"I'd like to purchase a small gift for my music tutor."

"Might I could help. A lot of musicians and teachers stop in here."

Gloria hadn't thought of that. Colin probably did frequent the store. She wondered briefly if she might have seen him here in the past without knowing who he was. "His name is Colin McDougal."

The clerk's face lit up. "Oh yes! I know Colin! He plays at the pub a few blocks over."

A twinge of jealousy twisted inside her gut. Miss Harding sounded rather familiar about Colin.

The bright friendliness in Miss Harding's eyes cooled slightly. "You are Miss Palmer, then?"

"I am. I thought a piece of sheet music should do." Hopefully, it would be enough to assuage her embarrassment at herself and her friends on how they treated him on Saturday. She wasn't looking forward to this afternoon's practice session with it unresolved.

"You don't know Colin very well, do you?" Tamara said, scrutinizing Gloria.

"No. Not well."

"He just has to hear a tune, and he can play it. He doesn't need sheet music. At least not for something short."

"He is very talented. But I thought...perhaps...there would be something..." She blew out a breath. "I really must make amends for an unfortunate incident between us."

Tamara raised her brows slightly and tilted her head as if trying to decide what might work. "A box from New York City arrived in yesterday's post. I haven't had time to put any of it out for display. Wait here." She walked through a curtained doorway, disappearing into a back room. When she returned, she carried the box and set it on the counter between them. "Let's have a look."

Together they dug through the contents. The newest sheet music from T.B Harms Publishing soon spread out before them. "Ah — How about this one?" Tamara asked, holding up the music for *Widdicombe Fair*.

Gloria flipped through the four pages. It was a simple arrangement compared to the classics that she played. "He'll have this done in no time."

She put it aside and continued searching. A moment later she came across Tchaikovsky's Piano Concerto No. 1. "This might do."

"I haven't heard him play that sort of music before...usually just the short, fun pieces at the pub."

Tamara looked doubtful that Colin would like it, but it was the type of music Gloria had played all along. Gloria kept digging through the box, carefully taking music out and setting it on the counter. Toward the very bottom of the box, she came across three packages of lined music paper.

"What do you think of this?" she asked the clerk. "He composes his own tunes. I wonder if he'd like this?"

Tamara smiled and nodded. "He usually lines his own paper. He will surely like that."

Gloria smiled. "I'll take it."

Tamara wrapped it up in brown paper and tied it with twine.

Once again, on the way out the door with her purchase, the leather satchel caught Gloria's eye. Perhaps…if she won the competition…

She hurriedly climbed into the waiting coach. She would have just enough time to have luncheon with Mother and then warm up at the piano to be prepared for when Colin arrived.

At one o'clock that afternoon, Colin strode into the music room, intent on getting through the lesson as best he could. It had become obvious to him, in the days since Saturday, that Welbourne and the others had had a good laugh at his expense. He'd learned his lesson — people on this side of the trolley tracks led a different life than they did where he came from.

He was determined to have no further thoughts of Gloria beyond their bargain. This was a business arrangement, and that was all. There was no way they could even be friends. All they had in common was their love for music, and that wasn't enough to overcome the difference in their status. Once the lessons were done, they would go their separate ways as though they had never known each other.

He slapped down his music folder on the chair. Where was she anyway? He looked about the room. The piano was opened and ready. He walked over to the instrument and touched the keys. Warm. She'd been here only moments ago. The tips of his fingers tingled. He rubbed them on his pants to wipe away the sensation.

A brown paper package sat in place of any music on the piano's music stand. Written in a flourish of black ink across the front of it was his name.

He picked it up. Turned it over.

"It's a peace offering," Gloria said from the open doorway. "I hope you will accept it."

He looked again at the package, then put it back on the music stand. "What is it?"

"A...peace offering."

"What for?"

"I feel terrible about what happened Saturday."

"Nothing happened." His voice was flat. "Let's get on with the practice session. I've got to leave early today." He didn't, but it was the first thing that popped into his mind.

She walked up to him. "George had no right to treat you like that."

He wasn't about to admit that he was bothered by any two-toned peacock. "That's the man you plan to marry?" he said, his jaw tight.

"Eventually. Although with you he showed a side of himself I have not seen before."

Colin lifted his chin. "That should tell you something."

"Perhaps." She began strolling about the room as she spoke. "I wish I could talk to him about music, the way I do with you. He doesn't understand how important it is to me. In that way, he is much like my mother. I tried to explain it once"—she smiled slightly—"and came away with the thought that it was like trying to explain snow to someone in Florida. He didn't understand at all."

Colin watched her move around the room as she spoke. Her gracefulness as she walked pulled him. He couldn't take his eyes off her — the gentle sway of her hips, the swish of her long olive-green dress. "Then why are you considering him?"

"We are compatible in other ways. And he would take good care of me."

"You didn't say that you love him."

She stopped short, her eyes widening with indignation. "My feelings for George are none of your business."

"I just wonder how much you'll play the piano after you marry him. Music gets inside you. It calls to your soul, your essence, the part of you that is closest to God. And he can't even understand that. How can he understand you?"

Her face reddened. "A note is a note."

She hadn't contradicted him. Interesting. "What made you start piano lessons, Gloria?"

"My mother. Does that surprise you?"

"Yes."

"Mother believes it is an important attribute for a woman. It completes her education, making her more..."

He raised his brows. "Marriageable?"

"Yes." She smiled briefly. "However, I don't think she expected me to take to it to the exclusion of my other studies."

He could well-imagine that. "Does it bother you that your father has made you wait to marry?"

She seemed surprised that he'd changed the topic. Surprised...and relieved. "Well...yes. At first it did. Now, I find that I am enjoying our lessons —

much more than I ever did with Mr. Peers — and the weeks are rushing by much too fast."

"Then the waiting period has been a good thing."

"I suppose so."

Didn't she recognize what was happening? She had just admitted that she enjoyed her music more than she wanted to be with Welbourne.

"Father believes that George is a fine catch and as such, he will take this period of waiting like a gentleman. So far, Father has been right."

"But you certainly aren't going after Welbourne as deliberately as you are your music."

She frowned. "For your information, a woman does not chase after a man. It isn't done in polite company." She walked briskly to the piano and picked up the package. "It's not good manners to refuse a gift. Here."

She shoved it at him.

He grabbed onto the package before it fell to the floor. Guess he'd gotten a bit too personal. He should apologize. "Gloria..."

"We have work to do." She sat down on the bench and started in on her scales.

She pounded the keys a bit, not quite so fluid. When she looked up at him once, her gaze was troubled. Maybe she did recognize more than she let on.

But by the time she started on Schubert, she had relaxed and the practice ended up going well. It was as if their...discussion...had cleared the air between them and put them back on level ground. It probably was an illusion, but he'd take it for now.

At the end of their time together, Gloria walked him to the front door.

"Will you open your present now?" she asked. "I'd like to see if you like it."

"Why wouldn't I like it? It's from you."

"Some people take issue with anything and everything—even small gifts."

"I think that's your mother speaking."

She shrugged prettily. "She is hard to please. Everything comes easy to you, doesn't it?"

"Easy? I wouldn't call chopping ice blocks all that easy."

She smiled. "I suppose not. I guess I've never met someone as accepting as you are about...life."

"Then we are even. I've never met anyone so—" He stopped. The words that came to mind were frustratingly beautiful. He couldn't very well say that. "Never mind."

He pulled the package from beneath his arm and untied the twine. Removing the brown paper, he stared at the pre-lined paper in his hands. He'd been sure the gift would have something to do with music, but this meant so much more. It showed that she believed in him as a composer.

"Friends?" she asked, resting her hand on his wrist.

His skin burned beneath her touch. "Yeah, friends," he admitted, feeling the last vestiges of his anger melt away.

"Thank you."

The way she looked up at him, so close, made his mind go blank and his mouth go dry. At this distance, the light from the gas-lamp in the entryway flickered in her eyes and turned them into big pools of liquid green. Her skin was so smooth and pale and her lashes dark against it. He tried to swallow and couldn't.

She didn't seem to notice. "Have you ever tried to publish one of your songs?"

"New York wasn't interested."

"Oh." She thought for a moment. "Will you try again?"

"I might. When I'm done here."

"You'll let me know if you send something?"

She wanted to keep in touch after the audition? "If you'd like."

She nodded. "I'll see you Thursday." She let go of his wrist and turned back inside, closing the door softly between them.

He stared at the door knocker, barely seeing it. He'd arrived here intent on keeping things strictly business.

He thought about her gift. It was perfect. *She* was perfect. Too good to be true. Welbourne wasn't right for her. He would never appreciate the woman that Colin knew.

He frowned, turning away from the door and starting toward home.

He needed to remember who he was—who she was. Welbourne was an appropriate match and Colin was nothing more than her music tutor...who caught fire whenever she touched him.

CHAPTER EIGHT

Colin opened the spigot, filling the mug with beer full to the top and not spilling a drop. He had been doing this job for so long that he could do it blindfolded if he had to. The weight of the mug in his hand and the sound of the beer as it flowed in was all he needed to get it right. He handed it off to Mr. Flannigan, a regular customer of McDougal's Pub, who sat at the far end of the bar. He came once or twice a week to enjoy a pint before heading home to his wife. "Cheers to you, Mr. Flannigan."

"I hear you've been spending time at the Palmers' Palace lately," Tom Stryder said, coming up to the bar. "Sounds like a sweeter deal than the dinner club."

Colin grinned. Guess it was something of a palace compared to the pub...or the Tarkington Club, for that matter.

"Is that Gloria Palmer a sweet deal?"

The smile for his friend, faltered. He didn't want Tom talking about Gloria that way. "It's not like that, Tom. It's work. That's all."

Tom smirked, not believing a word he said. "The pay is good, though, right?"

He nodded. The pay was very good. A fair amount of coins still jingled in his pocket even after putting half of his pay in the family jar. He'd certainly earned it—Gloria's playing was improving. It had been only two and a half weeks since he'd been going to the Palmers', but something he couldn't quite figure out was happening there. An underlying tension seemed to pervade the mansion. In a way, the dramatic music 'fit' the atmosphere of the house. He had nothing against classical music, but a steady diet of the moody stuff was enough to make anyone crave something light and fun once in a while. He'd have to remember that...perhaps take some of his pub music to her place.

"Play us a tune, Colin!" Mr. Flannigan called out and wrapped his knuckles on the oak bar. He swiped the back of his meaty hand across his lips and beard, wiping off the foam that clung there from his beer. "Something with kick."

"Sounds like a fine idea," Tom said. "Once you poor me a glass."

Colin did just that, then checked that his da could handle the three patrons still waiting for their beers and slipped out of his apron. He sat down at his beat-up piano, kissed the first two fingers of his left hand and then, as he always did, transferred that kiss to the edge of the instrument. "What's your pleasure?"

"Give us *Where Did You Get That Hat*," Tom said. "Let's see if you remember a good Irish song after all that fancy stuff you've been a-playing."

Colin started playing the simple tune. He didn't need written music. He could feel the notes. He could also feel the energy level in the pub escalate as he moved from the first refrain to the chorus. As usual, Tom and Mr. Flannigan joined in and belted out the words in a contest to see who could sing it louder.

When that song was finished, Colin started up with another. A second time through the chorus and two men started dancing a jig in the corner of the pub, their beer sloshing over the sides of their mugs. His brother James lowered his shoulders and gave Colin a look that said, *Here we go again*. It was his job to clean up the room of any spills.

Colin understood. It had been his job before it was James's. But the music, the camaraderie, meant their friends were finding a moment of happiness in a world that could be less than welcoming. What did a few spilled drops amount to when compared to that?

He expelled a deep breath, the tightness that had settled in his chest over the past week, began dissolving. This was what music was all about...bringing people together. Letting off steam. Having fun.

At the thought, his hands froze above the keys.

"What are you stopping for?" Tom asked, coming to stand behind him. "Something wrong?"

"She doesn't have any fun," he murmured as the thought took hold of him. Naw, he told himself.

Impossible. Everyone had fun in some way. Gloria must do something. But what? What did Gloria do to blow off steam?

CHAPTER NINE

She had only two weeks left before the competition and here she was taking a stroll with George.

"It is too beautiful a day for you to stay inside," her mother had said when George arrived on their doorstep and asked for her.

The weather was indeed fine. With the winter sun streaming down on them, the temperature hovered just above freezing and puffy white clouds splotched the blue sky. The fresh, crisp air invigorated her as they strolled together to the park.

"I believe I deserve equal time," George had said in a vaguely amused tone as he walked beside her. He tucked her gloved hand more securely in the crook of his arm and patted it. "You spend all your time with that piano. I have every right to be jealous."

George? Jealous?

"However, I hate to think of myself so insecure as to harbor such a base emotion."

They walked along, sharing information about mutual friends and things that had happened over the holidays. He had much more to share than she did, as isolated as she now was with her constant practicing. She didn't bring up her music, however, because whenever she had said something about it in the past, he usually dismissed her words as mundane or irrelevant. He didn't understand how important music was to her, and he never would, so she kept quiet for the most part.

From the bank of the Potomac, they watched the ice flows break up in the middle of the river. It brought to mind the day she had stood in nearly the same spot and watched Colin wrestle with the large blocks of ice, heaving them onto his wagon, his face ruddy with exertion. She couldn't imagine George doing such hard work, and yet Colin managed it — not with ease — but with a steady determination and vigor she found fascinating.

"How go the lessons?" George asked.

"Fair," she said, surprised he'd asked. She didn't elaborate. No point to it.

"Only fair? When you practice night and day?"

"I've plateaued. I'm not sure Colin notices. His...music background is different than mine."

"It's still 'Colin', is it?" George said flatly. "Really?"

She didn't comment.

"I'm not surprised he doesn't notice. He's used to pub music, dear. He doesn't have the ear for subtle distinctions."

This from a man who knew little of music! "He has still been helpful. More so than Mr. Peers. I just don't know how to advance from this stage."

George turned toward her. "Then why continue? You are an amazing pianist as you are. You could stop right now if you want. You don't have to prove anything to anybody."

His words troubled her. Was that what this was about? She supposed that, in a way, it was. She wanted to prove to herself that she could place in the audition, that she was good enough. Was that wrong?

When she didn't answer him, he took her arm again and they started back to her house. "There is something I want to show you. We'll take a small detour."

"I really should get back, George. Colin will be waiting."

He scowled. "Let him wait. If I recall, you are the one paying him."

They walked another block, heading away from the river and past the end of the small shopping district of town. She couldn't help but think they were only a few blocks from Colin's family pub and home, the neighborhoods sectioned off from each other by the trolley tracks.

"Why have we come this way?" she asked.

He didn't answer immediately, but walked to the corner and then stopped before a large, two-story house. "Now. Tell me what you think."

"A house, George?"

Before her stood a lovely two-story brick house with a large stone porch for the entryway. On each side of the porch was a three-sided bay window with mosaic-stained glass in the top panes. At each gabled end of the pitched roof, small carved finials sat. Two brick enclosures on each end of the roof, offered up three chimneys apiece.

"I found out the owners are moving to Savannah in four weeks and want to sell. I know it's not the same as building exactly what you want, but I thought it would do for a year or two."

She could barely speak. "A house? This house? Oh...George! I love it!" And she did. It was lovely, and better yet, it was only two blocks away from her parents' house. Certainly her mother would approve. She squeezed his arm. "You thought of everything."

He smiled his most winning smile, his dimples showing beyond his perfectly trimmed dark mustache. "Then I can move ahead with the funds to secure it?"

Her head was spinning. This had come about so fast! "But I haven't even said yes to your proposal yet."

He drew a familiar small box from inside his silk vest. "Time is money. I came prepared."

She shook her head, a bit overwhelmed at his tactics. No wonder Father wanted him for his shipping company. George could be formidable when he wanted something. "You are very persistent and although I am tempted, according to my father, you are supposed to wait until February fourteenth."

"When the outcome will be the same...why wait?" he said smoothly.

"George!" She didn't want to be disagreeable. Why must he press her so?

He huffed out a breath. "I have every confidence that you will come to your senses and say yes before Valentines Day."

His confidence put her more on edge. "Perhaps there is a way, that if I am accepted to the conservatory, I could be your wife *and* I could continue with my music."

The good humor faded from his expression. "What gave you that idea?"

"Well…with your influence, you could persuade the directors to allow me to continue and still go ahead with our wedding at the same time."

"I expect you to be my wife and mistress of our home," he said, drawing his dark brows together. "*This* home. Certainly you may have your piano here. I know playing brings you joy. But you will have other duties, social obligations that will come first. There won't be time for running off to the conservatory. Or, for that matter, practicing every day the way you do now."

She froze.

He inclined his head. "Did you expect me to come to your concerts? Sit there for the evening?"

"You have done that a number of times at the house. I thought you enjoyed listening to me play."

"That was only so that I could get to know you, and you me. You can't expect me to continue with it after we wed. It would be a waste of my time! I have business to attend to."

Her chest tightened at his words. She couldn't answer. That was exactly what she had expected…to look out into the front row of the audience and see him sitting there, impressed, proud. However, the way he said it, he obviously thought the concept absurd. She knew she couldn't be married and attend the conservatory—it just wasn't done. But she'd still expected to be closely emmeshed in Barrington's music culture. "I...know you don't care much for my playing, but, yes, I did think that."

"You cannot be serious, Gloria. I thought once you saw the house, you would give up this ridiculous notion."

"It isn't ridiculous."

He pressed his lips together. "I thought the point was to place in the audition and that was as far as this was going. That's what you said. That you wanted the validation."

"But what good does it do to win if I will not attend the conservatory?"

"According to an earlier conversation we had, that was never an option. I thought we were getting married." He squeezed her hand and gave a small shake of his head. "Perhaps here in the middle of the street isn't the best place to have this discussion."

The desire to argue deserted her. Her thoughts were churning with all that he had just said. She had assumed that they wanted the same things, with the exception of her love of music. She hadn't thought that chasm so very hard to cross. But speaking to him now, it became clear that he had an entirely different view of their future together. It was a life any of her friends would clamor to have. A life her mother had groomed her for. Only, she wasn't sure she wanted it now. She had to think about whether the life he offered—the beautiful house, the beautiful life, the security—was a life she truly desired.

When they arrived back at the house, Colin was waiting in the entrance, sitting on a marble bench made for that purpose. He held a folder on his lap and she wondered if he might have brought some of his own music. Her mother stood across the small space, an undercurrent of tension emanating from her. Apparently, they had been talking.

"I'm sorry I'm late," Gloria said, quickly removing her hat and handing it, along with her cloak, scarf and mittens to Mr. Ross. "Thank you for the lovely walk, George."

"I'll come by for you on Saturday."

"I look forward to it," she said, out of politeness, more than truthfulness.

George gave Colin a dark look before closing the door behind him. The room was starkly quiet as the sound of his footsteps on the walk outside faded away..

"Mr. McDougal, please wait in the music room. I believe you know the way by now. My daughter will be with you directly."

Gloria glanced at her mother. What now?

Beside her, Colin nodded and then turned and strode down the hall.

"Gloria? Come with me."

She followed her mother into the library. "What is it?"

"I just want to ask after your walk with George. You were a bit resistant to the idea this morning when you left. I hope all went well." She watched Gloria closely, as if searching for a hint of her mood.

Gloria had to sort through their conversation first. Too much had been said to go into it now with her mother. "We can talk about it later. I have to practice now."

Her mother waved that off. "Don't you think you should forget about this audition? You've had four weeks and by your own admission, you are not advancing as much as you would like in your technique. Perhaps this is it. You've given it a good try. But, there really is no need to continue. Didn't George say something to that effect?"

"He doesn't care to talk about my music. I know it sounds odd, but sometimes I get the feeling that he wants me to fail."

"Oh, don't be silly. He simply wants this all behind you so that you can settle down once and for all. You know he asked me what parts of Europe you were interested in. It sounds like he is considering an extended honeymoon there."

It was too much to cope with. First George and now her mother. Pushing. Prodding. Pressing her. "Mother. Please. We can talk about this later. Believe me, I truly do want to hear all that you have to say, but I'm late as it is for my practice session."

Her mother snapped her mouth closed. "Very well. Of course you mustn't keep that boy waiting. He has only so much time before he must get back to his real job…bartending."

She said it with such disdain, fairly spitting the word, that Gloria was taken aback. It wasn't like her mother to be so uncharitable.

"We will talk later this evening. When your father returns from work."

Gloria turned and rushed down the hall to the music room, escape the only thought filling her mind.

Once inside the room, she shut the doors tight and leaned her forehead against the cool wood. Just for a moment. Just until she could calm down. This was her sanctuary. Her special place. She had to block out all the tension on the other side of the portal.

Lord, what should I do? I want to make Mother proud. But why is it so hard? Everything I do is criticized or simply wrong. A sob shuddered through her with her effort to hold in her frustration.

"Gloria?"

She caught her breath. She hadn't forgotten that Colin waited in the room. She just couldn't attend to him with all the other going on. "I...just need a minute." She looked over her shoulder.

He took a step toward her and then stopped. Concern etched his features.

She had to get herself back in control. She swallowed. "It's all right. I'm all right."

He didn't move, simply waited.

She concentrated on her breathing. Inhale. Exhale. In. Out. Calm. Think...calm.

"She makes this hard for you," he said slowly.

She smiled faintly. "She means it for my good."

He didn't say more.

She blew out a shaky breath. "Well. Should we start?"

"Take a moment to warm up. You were out all morning."

She didn't hear censure in his voice. He was just stating a fact. "Mother thought I needed a break. She thinks I have been working too hard."

"Maybe you have. Maybe you put too much on yourself to win. What do you do for fun, Gloria? How do you let off steam?"

She should correct him. It wasn't professional or his place as her tutor to ask about personal things. He had been doing that more and more.

"Why...play the piano, of course," she said. "We had a lovely walk to the park and now I am ready to attend to my lesson."

His gaze narrowed on her. "Fair enough." He withdrew a few pieces of sheet music from his folder. "Let's start with the second piece of music, Heller's La Favorita."

"You have your own copy?"

"Yes," he said distractedly without glancing up.

"I'm just surprised. It isn't the type of music you usually play."

"I wanted to be prepared for today."

His answer couldn't have surprised her more. He had continually surprised her since the first time she met him. He understood and appreciated music innately, even the classical pieces she played that were so different from his realm of experience until now. How could Mother not appreciate this man's gift for the piano?

He glanced up when he realized she wasn't playing. "Are we starting?"

She settled on the piano bench and began her scales to warm up her fingers. She moved on to Heller's piece. As she played, she waited for the peace to come—that sense of well-being she usually felt as the music took hold of her. Today it evaded her. Her fingers found the wrong notes at the wrong time. She couldn't work the stiffness out of her hands. The sound was forced, foreign, ugly. She held the last chord, knowing that Colin would not be pleased with her rendition of the piece, and braced herself for his critical remarks.

She looked up.

Colin studied her in that way she was beginning to recognize—his head slightly tilted to the side, his blond lock of hair sweeping down and almost hiding one eye. After a moment, he rose and walked over to the piano. "Music isn't only about playing a note for every one that is written on a staff. It's about the mood the composer was trying to portray."

"Yes, yes, we've spoken of this before." Why did he feel the need to repeat himself unless he was preparing to criticize her? She didn't know if she could handle one more disparaging comment today.

"Technically, your playing is fine. But something is still missing."

"Well, I hope we will figure it out before the competition. We have only two weeks left." Her tone sounded churlish, even to her ears.

"Are you worried that you'll lose?"

"If I don't play perfectly? Yes, of course."

"So you are focusing on perfection, and if it's not, then it will be utter failure." His brow furrowed with concentration.

"I can't envision winning, not with all that is happening."

"Hmm."

"What do you mean...'hmm'?" Her voice sharpened in frustration.

He shrugged. "Maybe your mother is right. Maybe you do need a break."

"I don't have time to take a break!"

"At the beginning of all this, you said how important it was to be honest with each other, yet you are not being honest with me now." He leaned toward her. "Gloria...You are not even sure what you are going to do once you win."

How could he think that? Of course, she was sure. She very nearly hated him at that moment for pressing her. Her chest was tight with it. He was too critical, speaking to her too familiarly, and pushing her—always pushing her. The control she had on her temper began to slip.

"It's...complicated, what with Mother and with Mr. Welbourne...and Father too."

"Right," he said, his voice flat. "They know what they want. But you? It sounds like you don't know your own mind. If I'm right, then no matter how much you practice, it will be futile. On one hand, you are your own worst critic, and on the other hand, you sabotage yourself."

Why couldn't he just try to understand? There was no possible way she could answer him. "Stop. Please stop!"

He shook his head. "You wanted honesty. This is me being honest."

"It's just..."

"Just what?" he pressed further, his voice sharp.

"It's just that no matter what happens, someone I love will end up unhappy." It felt like all the air was sucked out of the room at her words. She cupped her hand over her mouth, shocked that she'd actually said what she was feeling out loud. How had she let that slip out? It was personal. Even thinking it scared her, because there was no solution—and she wanted there to be a solution.

He took a step toward her and then stopped, drawing his hands to his sides, curling them into fists.

She felt numb and shaky and exposed. She wished she'd never gotten out of bed that morning. The entire day had been a constant battering, and she was tired of it. "Please…I know you are trying to help. You…just can't understand."

He didn't move. "I think I do now. You put too much on yourself. You can't live your life for everybody else. In the end, you won't make anybody happy."

Instinctively, she knew that what he said was true. Why was it so hard for her to believe it inside? The concern on his handsome face was nearly her undoing. The urge to rush into his arms—to be held and comforted—overwhelmed her. But she was a Palmer.

And he was a bartender.

She closed her eyes. Frozen. Miserable inside. It was all hopeless. Maybe she should give up. George certainly wanted that. Her mother too.

Colin's footsteps sounded behind her. "Scoot over."

Her eyes flew open.

"Make room for me on the bench."

She did as he asked.

He set an unfamiliar piece of music on the piano's music stand. She glanced through the two pages. "This looks like something you would play at your tavern. How can this help with preparing for the audition?"

"It probably can't."

"Colin. This is a bit irregular, don't you think?" She felt the urge to stand up, to put space between them.

"We played a duet that first time I was here. What's so different now?"

It was different. He was no longer a stranger, and he, of all people, seemed to understand how important music was to her. "Let me try that last piece again."

"You won't play it any differently than before."

She didn't want him to know how poorly she played compared to him in a situation like this. "I'm not very good at sight reading," she said, hedging.

"I don't care. Make all the wrong notes you want. I just want you to bang away on the piano until you get to the other side of whatever is bothering you. Until you get it out, it is going to eat at you and affect your practice."

She stiffened. "A person doesn't just 'bang away' at an instrument. Besides, nothing is bothering me except for not being prepared for the audition."

He grinned. "Then prove it. Play this. We're not going back to the other piece until you do."

She let out a long-suffering sigh. "You can be overly bold at times, Mr. McDougal."

His grin only grew bigger.

She placed her hands on the keys and started in. The music was simplistic and in the key of C. After playing it through once without a mistake, she dropped her hands in her lap. "There. Done. Now can we get back to business?"

Colin shook his head. "Play it again. This time in the key of G."

After that, he asked for it in the key of D. With each progression, he asked for a key that added more sharps until she was playing primarily on the black keys. She was feeling quite pleased with herself. The tune was simple enough that she was able to perform each new version without mistakes.

"Not bad," he said when she finished.

"Not bad? I think it was a far cry from 'not bad.'"

His grinned. "Now keep up with me."

He started with the key of G, playing the ditty faster, the lower notes slightly louder than any of her renditions. She joined in two octaves above him playing the same notes that were written. The next time through he played his part as a round like *Row, Row, Row Your Boat*. And then again, a little faster.

She kept up, beginning to enjoy the competition, entirely focused on their hands, his larger and hers, so much smaller, flying over the keys. He would play softer, so she played softer. He would play louder, so she played louder. Then he changed from that. He no longer played the notes as they were printed on the paper, but created chords and runs while still keeping to the essence of the tune.

She made a mistake—quite noticeable—and glanced up to see if he noticed. He raised his brows, but otherwise just kept on playing. All right then, she would show him! She increased the speed, challenging him. He kept going and then went ahead of her. He was trying to trip her up! The cad!

"And now for the finish…" he said at the height of the din and played a resounding chord as the ending, each finger occupying a key.

She laughed. "There is no way that my hand will stretch that far. You have the advantage with your big clumsy hands."

"Clumsy! No one has ever said that to me before." But he chuckled, his blue eyes twinkling.

"Here. Hold up your left hand."

He did.

And she placed her right hand against his. Her fingertips only reached to the last knuckle of his fingers. "See?"

Warmth invaded her palm and raced up her arm to her cheeks.

The mirth she'd seen on his face evaporated as his gaze locked onto hers. He swallowed.

Her heart beat faster. In that instant, she became aware that her shoulder rubbed against his and his thigh pressed against hers. Suddenly he wasn't her tutor or someone that she'd hired. He was…more.

Shaken at the thought, she withdrew her hand and looked away from his penetrating gaze.

She stared at the ivory keys before her. "You are a poor one to talk about going after what you want, Colin. Look at you. You possess more talent in your little toe than I do in my entire body, and yet you slave away at that pub. I'm not the one who should be auditioning. It should be you."

"Gloria..." he said. "I—"

The sound of footsteps firing rapidly down the hall made her scoot off the bench and stand apart from him. Her heart raced.

Mother pushed through the doors and glared at them both. "What in heaven's name is happening in here? What was all that noise!"

Colin stood. "An experiment, Ma'am."

"Well, I hope that is the end of it. My daughter is a concert pianist, not some common street performer. My head will be throbbing for the next two days with that pounding!"

"It won't happen again, Mother."

"See that it doesn't." With a stern look at Gloria and then at Colin, she added, "And you will keep the doors open at all times. Understood?" She didn't wait for acknowledgment but swept out of the room as quickly as she had entered.

Gloria was mortified. "I'm...so sorry, Colin."

"What for?"

She rubbed her forehead. "I don't know. For my poor playing earlier? For Mother's tirade just now? For wasting your time? It seems there's always something to be sorry for." She lowered her hand. Now that Mother had left, she could think more clearly. "I...was having fun," she admitted. "Your tavern music"—she searched for the right word— "is a delight."

He smiled. "Good, then it accomplished what I intended. You loosened up. You relaxed. Had fun."

"You know," she said. "I meant what I said earlier. You don't belong there. At the pub."

He snorted softly. "It's my da's pub. Our family pub. Sure I belong there. Where else would I be?"

"At the conservatory. Writing your music for everyone to hear...not just Tarkington's Dinner Club."

An amused twinkle came into his blue eyes. "My music isn't the type for Marlowe. And New York isn't interested either. Besides, my family needs me at the pub."

"Then you are hiding your own light."

"This isn't about me," he said seriously. "I'll give one hundred percent to make your dream come true, Gloria. You deserve it with all the work you've put in. But you are the only one who can figure out what that dream is."

He walked to the piano and gathered his sheet music, stuffing it into his folder.

The image of his fingers touching hers came to mind, and then the intense look that had been in his eyes. Would she ever be able to forget that?

"Colin?" She couldn't let him leave without letting him know how much his words...his friendship...meant to her. She walked up to him and placed her hand on his sleeve. "Thank you."

His blue gaze traveled from her hand on his arm to her face. In it she saw strength and determination. "You can win. You are ready."

"That's not what I mean. Thank you for caring...enough to let me make up my own mind. It means more than you know."

He covered her hand with his for a long moment, his warmth permeating her all the way to her core. Then he stepped away, took hold of his satchel and walked to the door.

"My brother and I need to get one more load of ice on Saturday. We like to skate a bit before we get down to working hard."

She went still. "Are you asking me to join you?

"Just letting you know is all."

She listened to the sound of his boots on the wooden floor until she heard the front door closing behind him.

CHAPTER TEN

Saturday morning, Gloria was still undecided about meeting Colin at the park. She had been unable to think about anything else since he told her that he would be there. It wasn't an invitation—that would be presumptuous of someone of his station. And yet...why else would he have told her? Her stomach churned with indecision.

On awaking to a windy, mildly sunny day, she dressed in her forest-green riding skirt, forgoing her bustle in order to have more freedom of movement to skate. She was still conflicted. Perhaps if Sandra accompanied her, she would go skating. Her cousin loved to do things out-of-doors. It was a shame that they could not get together more often, but with Gloria's own rigorous practice schedule, outings fell by the wayside.

Sandra lived three blocks from the center of town and the park. When Gloria knocked on her door, her cousin was quick to agree. As she waited for her to gather her skates and coat, Gloria felt a twinge of guilt for not being completely honest with her, but…there was the possibility that Colin would not show up. If he did, she would simply act as though the meeting was by chance. Colin was a friend. That's all. Still, saying that to herself did nothing to dampen the buzzing sensation going through her as she walked briskly along the walk by the river, her skates dangling from her hand.

A thrill of excitement shot through her. She wasn't doing anything wrong, but in the back of her mind she knew Mother would not approve. If only Tad were here. Her brother would laugh at her way of thinking that this was so naughty…like a secret assignation. He had always been bolder than Gloria. What she wouldn't give to talk to him about all that was happening in her life. He would like Colin.

She and Sandra passed by the area on the river where she had seen Colin cutting ice a week before. He wasn't there, and so they continued to the frozen lake at the park. Taking a seat on one of the wrought-iron benches, they put on their skates. The place was busy with several children and their laughter and yelling filled the crisp air. An older couple, holding hands, glided sedately along the ice at the far end.

"Ready?" Sandra asked. She was one year younger than Gloria and would probably skate circles around her.

Gloria hunched over, struggling to tighten the skates onto her shoe. "In a minute. The key is being difficult."

"Here, let me try," Sandra said.

"It worked fine last weekend. I don't know what the trouble is."

A shadow fell across her lap.

"May I help?" a deep voice asked.

Gloria straightened up so fast she nearly knocked her head against Sandra's chin. "Hello, Colin...Mr. McDougal. I would invite your help." Beside him, stood James.

"Sandra, may I present my music tutor, Colin McDougal and his brother James McDougal. This is my cousin Sandra."

"Hello," Sandra said and colored prettily when James winked at her.

Colin took the key from Sandra and knelt with one knee on the ground. As he fixed Gloria's skate securely to her boot, she studied his wayward hair, thick and blond, that stuck out from the rim of his stocking cap. A dark-blond dusting of whiskers coated his jaw and upper lip, making him look very manly. He usually was clean shaven on his visits to her house.

"Done," he said, and released her foot. He assisted her to her feet. "We'll see you on the ice."

She walked with Sandra to the rink's edge and stepped out onto the ice.

"Who are those two?" her cousin asked the minute they were away from Colin and James. "And don't think I didn't see the way you looked at that blue-eyed boy."

"He's not a boy," Gloria said. "He's my piano tutor."

Sandra arched one dark brow. "You expect me to believe that?"

"I do. And, I might add, I noticed you blush when James winked at you."

Sandra's brown eyes danced with merriment. "It was improper of him...but I couldn't act shocked if I tried. He is so very pleasant-looking."

Gloria had butterflies in her stomach as she pushed off with her cousin, keeping to the outer edge of the ice. Although she was steady, Sandra at her side helped to make her more sure of herself. Children rushed past, so bundled up for warmth and so close to the ice that when two boys ran into each other and fell, they barely noticed it, but scrambled back up on their short legs and raced on.

One turn around the ice and suddenly Colin came up behind her to her side. He held out his hand to her, a challenge in his eyes. Without hesitation, she released her grip on Sandra and took hold of his. Sandra opened her mouth to speak, only to have James shoot past and challenge Sandra to a race. A delighted grin spread across her face, and she took off after him.

The next two hours passed by in a blur. Gloria could not remember having so much fun or laughing so much. They glided four abreast, crisscrossing their feet, and then Colin and James would swing her and Sandra around to skate backward while they still held on. Colin left her side only twice, to race his brother to the far end of the lake and back, coattails flying, barely winning each time.

At noon, clouds rolled in and covered the sun. The wind kicked up and the temperature dropped. When she breathed in it felt like the moisture in her throat turned to droplets of ice. The children hurried off to their homes, and Gloria knew it would be wise to go too, but she hated for the fun to end. Winded and ruddy-cheeked from his last race with James, Colin sat down beside her on the bench while James and Sandra took a turn around the frozen lake once more.

"Next year, he'll beat me," he said as he breathed hard, drawing in air. "He gets faster every year."

"Sandra has always been a better skater than I am. It's so with anything out-of-doors." She sighed, watching them show off, skating backwards and then sideways, heading farther down the ice. "It makes me miss my brother to watch you have such fun with yours."

She looked back at him and noticed a wet leaf that stuck to his wool cap. "How did this get here?" She reached up to pluck it out. He leaned forward slightly to accommodate her, and when he straightened, he slid his arm behind her to rest on the back of the bench. He had drawn close enough that she could feel the heat emanating off his body. It made it difficult to think straight.

She glanced down the lake to look for James and Sandra. They were mere specks in the distance at the far end of the lake.

"I didn't know you had a brother." His voice was low, intimate.

Shivers raced through her and her pulse quickened. "Tad is in Oregon now. He left when I was eleven."

"Why did he leave? Seems he could have had one heck of a future here with your father's company."

"He…he didn't want to use Father's company as a step up. He wanted to make his own mark. He and

Father butt heads often, each expecting the other to see things his way."

"So he left…" Colin studied her face, and then he slipped his gloved hand around the back of her neck.

She swallowed. Her skin tingled under his glove, feeling at once the cold crystals of ice and the heat that emanated through the wool to melt them. She shivered again. He was so close that their noses practically touched. "Colin…What are—"

"…and took all the family gumption with him."

"I have gumption," she said breathlessly, looking up into his warm gaze.

He smiled, his eyes crinkling at the corners. "I believe you do." And with that he leaned down and kissed her.

His lips were warm and soft and his stubble of whiskers scratched her cheek. Her heart fluttered in her breast. He was tender with her. A sweetness swept through her at the thought. He kissed her as though he cherished her.

And yet this wasn't proper. She was practically engaged! She should…

He pulled back, looking slightly dazed. The kiss had affected him as much as her. "I've thought about doing that ever since you first played for me."

A nervous giggle bubbled up. "That long ago?"

A slow grin spread across his face.

He rose to his feet and stepped backward onto the ice. He held out his hand, beckoning. "One more turn about the ice, Miss Palmer?"

She stood and placed her hand in his, letting him draw her, gliding across the ice and into his arms.

Colin sat at the bar and hunkered over the lined pages Gloria had given him. It was late, but until he got down a small semblance of the melody that clamored inside him, he wouldn't be able to sleep.

"Are ye startin' a new one?"

Ma rested her hand on his shoulder a moment as she watched. Then she moved the kerosene lantern closer. "Fancy paper there. Must be makin' good money working for Miss Palmer."

He grunted, making a quick treble clef on the page. He'd been waiting all evening for the pub to clear of customers so he could get to this. The song had been clattering around in his head ever since he'd kissed her...and she hadn't slapped him.

Pa turned the key in the lock and pulled the blinds. "Are you ready to go up, Mrs. McDougal?"

Colin was vaguely aware of his mother taking his father's hand.

"See that you save some of yourself for tomorrow, boy-o," Da said. "We'll be going to early Mass. And don't forget to put out the light before coming up to bed."

Ma kissed Colin on the forehead lightly.

As his folks headed toward the stairs, Colin heard Ma chide his Da, "He's old enough to know all that! And he's too old for you to be calling him boy-o."

Da chuckled. "He'll always be me boy, Ma." He said something more as they disappeared up the stairs. Colin couldn't make it out and didn't try. He drew the bass clef. Then the time. He'd start the music in six-eight time.

He started jotting down notes and rests as fast as he could, as fast as the tune took shape in his head. The first ten bars came easily. He could hear the notes inside himself, hear the way they needed to be played. He wrote quickly to get them down on paper before they floated away, lost forever. He would come back later and embellish them by adding chords, grace-notes, and such.

His hand began to cramp. He shook it out, then stretched it against his thigh. And kept going. His pencil wore away until it was nothing but wood scraping paper. He pulled his pocket-knife from his back pocket and reformed the tip. And he kept going—feverishly. Ten more bars. Another ten. This had happened before. Inspiration came to him in the most unlikely of places. A cat's meow. The lilt of his mother's voice calling to James. A woman's kiss. If he heeded its pull, honored it with his complete presence, a work of substance almost always happened. Only a few times had he had to crumple up the pages he had written and throw them away.

Finally, when his pencil needed shaping again, his eyes burned with fatigue, and his fingers refused to loosen up from their clenched position, he stopped.

He felt drained...tired. Satisfied. There before him was the essence of the melody. He gathered up the papers and carried them to the piano, itching to play it.

The first notes he played softly, so as not to wake his family sleeping above on the second story. He soon forgot about them and got lost in the song. Usually, his songs were quirky and fun. Sometimes they were a bit raucous even. Great for the pub. But this one was completely different than anything he'd ever written before. It started out soft and flowing. It had elements of a classical piece of music, but not quite. Gradually, a lush, sweeping, romantic melody emerged.

As he played, it was as though he could feel God's pleasure. And now, thinking over the events of the past three weeks, he could see God's hand in all that had happened. Things had lined up...playing at the dinner club, catching Gloria's attention, her father's firing of her past music teacher. It had forced him to be immersed in classical music — something he never before had given much thought to — and it had changed the way he heard all music. He came to the last note and closed his eyes. His soul, his heart, were full. He breathed out a prayer of thanks.

It needed more work. This was a rudimentary form of what he heard in his head, but now that it was down on paper, he could make it better. And when he was finished, he would play it for Gloria. No one at the pub ever thrilled at listening to or discussing music the way she did. It was a new experience for him. Sharing his passion for music.

He stared at the notes before him and realized something. This was her song. She was the inspiration. It captured her soul like the ebb of the tide, from the moment he met her when she was cool and aloof, up to today when he had kissed her and her eyes had gone all soft.

What had possessed him to do that? He was sure after some thought, she would regret the entire moment. He hoped it didn't make the rest of their time together awkward because he wanted more than anything to see her win the competition. She was so close. So very close to the two pieces being perfect.

He'd given a lot of thought to the waiting period Gloria's father had instigated. He had immense respect for Stephen Palmer. He was sure the man knew his own daughter better than any of them. By making both George and Gloria wait until the audition, he was giving Gloria time to figure out for herself what she wanted her future to be.

Colin only wished he could be a part of it, foolish though that thought might be.

A light tapping sound came from the front of the pub, at the window. Standing there, his nose pressed against the glass, was his cousin, Patrick. When Da had argued with him and sent him on his way, it was the middle of summer and the weather still warm. Now, he stood with his shoulders hunched against the cold and he gripped the collar of his woolen coat, keeping it closed to protect his neck. No scarf...no hat.

Colin strode to the front door and opened it, careful not to make too much noise and wake his parents. "Come in, Patrick. Warm yourself."

His cousin shook his head. "Not on your life. Uncle Shaun made it clear I wasn't welcome."

"What have you been doing, then? Where are you staying?"

"I'm helping out at Gunter's place for now. There's a room in the back where I sleep."

Colin frowned. Patrick had always been proud that the brew he made at Mcdougal's was rich and full-bodied. Hans Gunter was known for watering down his beer. "That's no place for you. You are family. You've got as much right to be here as I do."

Patrick snorted. "Tell that to your da."

"He'll change his mind."

"Looks like he is getting along fine without me."

"No. He's slowing down. That business this summer and then the fight with you took something out of him."

Patrick lowered his gaze. "I'm sorry about that. It's me and my quick temper. I don't expect he'll be forgiving me very soon." He looked back at Colin. "I only came to let you know where I was in case...well...in case things change. I'll be going now." He backed away.

"Your only fault is that you cared enough to stand up to Da. You both wanted what was best for McDougals. There's no shame in that." Colin stretched out his hand.

Patrick looked at it and then grasped it hard.

Colin stared after him as he trudged away, disappearing into the dark cold night.

CHAPTER ELEVEN

Monday morning, James stood on the flatbed and maneuvered the heavy barrels filled with beer to the wagon's edge. There, Colin took the barrel onto his shoulder and strode into the back storage room of the pub. He lowered the heavy barrel carefully to the ground and then positioned it in line with the ten barrels he had already set down against the wall. Then, he hoisted an empty barrel onto his shoulder and strode back to the wagon to hand it to James.

Drops of perspiration trickled down his brow despite the cold. He shucked his coat and found his shirt sticking to his back because of his sweat. Over and over he repeated the process with the barrels. Their profits were down since they had to buy most of their beer from another company now rather than make their own. It would be this way until Da hired another master brewer or until he asked Patrick to come back. Colin had to find a way to make that happen. He thought about it more and more since Patrick's visit.

With only five barrels to go, Da came from the front of the pub, a frown upon his face, and his focus on Colin. Behind Da, strode George Welbourne.

Colin straightened.

"I'll have a word with you, McDougal."

Colin glanced at James. "Take a break. We'll finish this in a minute."

"This won't take that long," Welbourne said, his fists clenched, his stance that of a man looking for trouble.

"Have you come to fight, then?"

"No." He uncurled his fists. "I wouldn't soil myself with your sweat."

On the way to going inside, James stopped. He crossed his arms over his chest and leaned against the doorframe. "Think I'll stay."

"Suit yourself," Welbourne said.

"What's this about?" Colin asked, although he thought he might know—Gloria. Somehow the man had found out about their time at the park.

"You have been helping yourself to something that is mine."

"And what is that?"

"My fiancée.

"But she is not your fiancée yet."

"She might as well be. I've bought a house and I plan to take her as my wife just as soon as this farce of a competition plays out."

Colin walked up to stand before Welbourne. They stood nose to nose, the same height, although where Welbourne was thin from working a job behind a desk, Colin carried more bulk. "I'm curious. What made you agree to it?"

Welbourne chuckled mirthlessly. "I wouldn't expect you to understand a gentleman's agreement."

Colin studied him. "Or the fact that Palmer holds your pay. That might have something to do with it."

"You will never know." Welbourne pulled a rolled piece of paper from his inside vest pocket. "I've come to say that you need to stay away from Miss Palmer." He waved the paper as if it held some importance to Colin.

"What's that?"

"The loan on your pub here. I will call it in if you see her again."

Colin heart jolted in his chest and he glanced over at his father. "Let me see that."

Welbourne gave him the paper.

Colin unrolled it and glanced over the printed document.

"You will note that this is a copy. The bank has the original draft."

Welbourne's name, sprawled large as you please at the bottom, gave him ownership of the building's loan. This couldn't be happening.

"I did a little digging and came across Mr. Cook's paperwork from last summer. I persuaded him to sell the loan to me."

"Seems you've had a busy morning."

Welbourne smirked. "I know how to look out for my interests."

Colin blew out a breath as his situation became clear. He couldn't jeopardize the pub, but he didn't want to let Gloria down either. "She has four more practice sessions before the audition."

"Not with you she doesn't."

"I'll say a proper goodbye." He felt a weight pressing down on him. He didn't want to stop seeing her. He didn't want her marrying this man. "You don't care that you could ruin her chances."

"I want a wife. Her. I don't care if she wins or loses. I never did."

Colin's blood heated. "Please man. Let her have her chance."

Welbourne snatched the document from his hand. "Make tomorrow your last day. Tell her goodbye. I don't care what excuse you give her as long as you leave me out of it. After that, don't come within ten feet of her or I'll demand full payment on this loan." He smirked as he said the last and then strode through the door.

Colin met his brother's gaze.

"I didn't tell anyone about the other day," James said, backing up slightly.

"It doesn't matter. I'm not risking this pub."

James nodded slowly, his eyes narrowing on Colin. "You love her."

"Yeah, but that means nothing if it comes to Ma and Da losing this pub."

CHAPTER TWELVE

Colin knocked on the Palmers' front door on Tuesday at his regular time. The threat from Welbourne still rang in his ears, and he knew he'd have to be careful how he acted at today's lesson or Gloria would be the one to suffer. At this point, with only ten days to the competition, he couldn't do anything that would ruin her chances of winning.

He had finished the music he had written for her. He was proud of it. It was different than anything he'd ever written before, influenced heavily by the music he'd heard her play. This might be his only chance to give it to her. He hoped he could do it privately. He was sure Gloria's mother would not wish him to give Gloria anything to remember him by.

Mrs. Palmer opened the door and ushered him in. "Gloria is in the music room."

He nodded and started down the hall as he always did.

"Mr. McDougal!" Mrs. Palmer's voice rang out in a no-nonsense tone. "I will accompany you, if you please."

He stopped. An escort? After all the times that he'd gone on his own?

She walked up to him, holding herself stiff enough and her head high enough it was a wonder she didn't scrape the ceiling. "Before we go, may I caution you that I've been informed of some goings-on that are not acceptable. Mind you, I am on the precipice of whether you shall get any recommendation after your task here is completed. If you hope to take another music position anywhere in this town, you must tread very carefully. Do you understand what I'm saying?"

Frustration mounted inside as he listened to her. What he had shared with Gloria was a thing of beauty. He respected her. He loved her. The only thing he had done wrong was to be born to the wrong class and there was little he could do to change that. A man did the best he could with what he had. It was obvious by her stern look that Mrs. Palmer did not want to hear any of his explanation so he simply answered her. "As clear as glass."

She turned and led him down the hall, leaving the doors to the music room wide open as she walked through and announced, "Mr. McDougal is here."

Gloria was looking out one of the tall windows that faced the river. She turned at her mother's words and met his gaze. "Hello, Colin."

He was struck by Gloria's calm and distant attitude. He wasn't sure what he'd expected after the kiss they had shared, but it certainly included a bit more warmth toward him. What had happened? Gloria stood there, stiff and reserved to the point of appearing like an ice-princess. Her light-blue dress — silk, he thought — was the color of the frozen water in the park rink. Her skin against her deep auburn hair, looked pale, and dark shadows smudged a tired half-circle under her green eyes.

At her daughter's use of his given name, Mrs. Palmer pressed her lips together in displeasure. She cleared her throat.

"My mother will be joining us today," Gloria said. "She insists on it."

So much for a moment to talk things out. Didn't look like it was going to happen. Whether it was Welbourne or Gloria who had spoken up about Saturday, it didn't matter. He had learned his lesson. He didn't belong in their world and from what he'd witnessed inside these walls, he wouldn't want to. He frowned at the thought. Except Gloria had been raised here and, to him, she was perfection.

He pulled off his cap and gloves, then shrugged from his coat and draped it over a chair back. He put down his satchel beside the chair.

Gloria walked over to the piano. "I have two extra tickets. One is for you. And the other is for a friend if you have someone you would like to invite."

He smiled briefly and joined her. "I'll have to think on that one. Not too many of my friends are used to classical music."

"Tamara, perhaps?"

"Do you want me to bring her?"

Her gaze darted to her mother who stood listening. "It is entirely up to you. You are also welcome to sit with my family if you choose."

"Is Welbourne coming?"

"Of course," she said lightly, but her eyes begged him to understand something else.

He tried to ignore the tug of them.

Mrs. Palmer walked over to the row of chairs and sat down. It was clear that she would chaperone this last session.

"I'll probably stand in the back," he said. "I'll listen and watch the reactions of the judges." He took the tickets that she offered, feeling the slight tremble in her hand, and slipped them in his shirt pocket. Whatever had transpired here had upset her. And he was the culprit in the long run. How could he have known that he'd fall far and hard for a woman beyond his reach? A woman who would be as out of place at McDougal's as he was in this fine mansion?

He took a deep breath and then exhaled. Wondering about what could and couldn't be wouldn't help. "Let's get busy. There isn't much time left before the big event."

She slipped onto the bench. "I am starting to get nervous."

He could only do his best to bolster her up, but he was honest when he said, "No need to be. You are ready."

A mischievous smile played about her lips. "I'd feel better if we could play a hardy rendition of *Where Did You Get that Hat* to warm up."

A grin threatened. She was entirely too endearing. He'd miss her. A lot. "Maybe another time. If I remember, it gives your mother a headache."

"True." The sparkle left her eyes as she began concentrating on her scales. She was like a bird in one of those fancy cages — smart enough to open the door but so content with her pampering that she chose to stay. The audition was her one shot at opening that door. He hoped she recognized it when it opened — and didn't hesitate to step through.

She played through her first piece twice and had only one area that was a little rough. The judges might not even notice, and in ten days she'd have it mastered anyway. Mrs. Palmer watched him like a guard dog would watch a cat prowling below. Every time he leaned close to Gloria to turn the page for her, he felt her gaze on him.

Gloria finished playing with a flourish and put her hands in her lap, just as she should at the competition.

"Good job," he said. "Now for the next one."

Her mother cleared her throat. "I'll be back in just a moment. Please continue." She rose and stepped from the room.

Gloria let out a deep breath and looked up at Colin. He still sat too far away in his chair, even though it was nearly flush against the piano bench that she sat on. "That was difficult," she admitted. "I felt her censure the entire time I played."

The corner of his mouth quirked up. "Then she is probably good practice for you at this stage."

She loved that half-grin. It made her feel immediately at ease and she relaxed. Colin hadn't shaved as he usually did before their sessions. A stubble of darker blond beard covered his jawline. He must be very busy at his family's tavern. She didn't want to talk about her mother. She wanted to ask him how he felt about the kiss but wasn't sure how to bring it up in the conversation. "Mother means well."

"Why does she suddenly need to chaperone us?"

She raised her brows. "You have to ask? I came home Saturday after the park and George was waiting for me. I'd completely forgotten that he'd said he was coming by and that we were to go out for luncheon. It was obvious where I'd been since I was standing there holding my skates."

"Everyone forgets appointments now and then."

She shook her head. "Not when it is George. And Sandra didn't think to keep quiet. She spilled the entire thing before I could stop her."

He pulled back, a worried expression on his face. "She said something about our kiss?"

"She wouldn't ever mention something that personal, but she did say that she'd had a great time skating with James and that I had skated with you. I believe George gathered the rest from the look on my face." It had been awful. She hated to hurt George or her mother, and she knew that what she had done would do just that, yet she wasn't sorry for meeting Colin at the rink or for letting him kiss her. She could never be sorry for that. It changed everything for her.

He whistled under his breath, and then leaned toward her. He grasped her hands in his, his warmth radiating through her skin. "I didn't mean to cause trouble for you."

Worry and his apology shone in his eyes. He didn't need to say it. She could feel it in the way he held onto her. Just his touch calmed her, made her feel whole. She had to tell him...had to explain. "Colin...I..."

He sat up straight suddenly. "So that's what set Welbourne off. Now I understand why he came by the pub."

George came by the pub? "What are you saying? Has George said something to you?"

He grimaced slightly. "We had a talk. Cleared the air."

She could only imagine what might have transpired. Colin didn't sound as though he wanted to share more with her, but she had to know where things stood between them. Things had changed drastically with that kiss. At least for her they had. "What are your thoughts about" — she swallowed — "us?"

"Us? The first day I came here, you said that if I helped you, there was a good chance I would learn something from you while I was working with you. You were right. I have learned a few things. More than I expected."

"Like what?"

He shrugged. "Oh...like you've got more backbone than I expected."

"You are being evasive."

He blew out a breath. "Like the fact that I like classical music — which is more than I could say when I started out."

"You hadn't had much exposure to it. But that's not what I meant with my question." She avoided his gaze. She'd hoped he'd say that he had learned he liked her...as more than a student. That the kiss had meant something to him.

For a long, drawn-out moment, he looked down at the music he held in his hands. "I understood you, Gloria. We need to concentrate on the audition and nothing else," he said deliberately. "At this point you don't need any extra distractions to take your mind off your performance for the conservatory."

She pulled back, struggling to hide her disappointment. She had hoped he felt something special between them. She certainly had. "But...I thought...You kissed me, Colin."

His gaze cleared slightly. "I'm not sorry for kissing you, Gloria. Don't ever get that idea. Kissing you was...amazing. But I am sorry for the timing."

She felt her heart drop inside her. This was not how she expected this conversation to go at all! She wasn't sure what she wanted...but one thing was becoming more clear. She wasn't sure that Welbourne was the right man for her. She pressed her palm to her temple. "But...Colin..."

Her mother's footsteps echoed in the hallway. She was on her way back to the music room.

Disappointed that they couldn't speak of things more, Gloria scooted over to the middle of the piano bench.

"It's just until after the audition," Colin said.

He didn't understand. By then she would have had to make her decision. She wanted to know how he felt about her now because everything hung on that. "Certainly," she said, holding herself with as much dignity as she could muster. She met his gaze.

"Everything will be over once the audition is done. That's what all this practicing is for. Right?"

"It has been more than a job to me, Gloria. I think you know that. But you and I, we come from two different worlds. Except for music, do you honestly think there could be a place where we could meet in the middle?"

Yes! She wanted to cry out. There had to be. He was so much more than a music teacher to her.

Her mother strode into the room, measured the distance between them with her narrowed gaze, and then took her seat again. "Well? Am I to hear the second piece?"

Gloria fumbled with the papers on the music stand. Her eyes burned as she tried to hold herself together. It was her own fault that she expected so much with a man like Colin. Of course he had kissed other women. She remembered him saying something to James about a girl that first day she went to see him at McDougal's. And Tamara seemed to know him quite well. A kiss probably meant very little to a man as experienced as he was. Yet, for her, his kiss had left her breathless with its possibilities — possibilities of a future together. How naïve. She had been a fool. She had believed those possibilities were truly attainable.

Somehow she managed to make it through La Favorita. She knew it wasn't her best performance of it, but Mother wouldn't know that, and thankfully, Colin seemed to sense her mood and didn't say anything.

"I'll go through one more time," she said after they had discussed a few areas she could improve. She started again.

A loud knocking on the front door made her stop. The handle jiggled, loud enough for them to hear in the music room, and then the door slammed open with a bang.

"Colin! Colin! Where are you?" James yelled into the house. He sounded frantic. Then his footsteps sounded on the wooden floor as he raced down the hall.

Colin strode to the hallway. "What's wrong?"

James slid to an abrupt stop at the door. "It's Da! Come quick!"

Colin glanced back at Gloria. He looked stricken, his face washed of all color. Then, without a word he grabbed his coat, and raced down the hall.

CHAPTER THIRTEEN

She didn't hear from Colin after he'd raced out of the house on Tuesday. Wednesday came and went with no news either. Thursday, James delivered a note to the door that Mr. Ross intercepted and passed to her mother. Mother brought it to her in the solarium.

It was in Colin's handwriting. Gloria read it out loud.

Da collapsed. Doc says it is his heart. I have to tend to the business here.

Will try to make it to your audition. You are ready!

She lowered her hands, still holding the note, to her lap. Even in this crisis, Colin was thinking of her. She wanted to know more. How was Mr. McDougal fairing now? How was Colin handling everything...and James too? Her heart went out to the family. She knew that Colin could take care of business at the pub—there didn't seem to be anything he couldn't do—but how was he managing his father's illness? She wanted to see him...talk to him.

Mother watched her carefully...waiting for a response.

"He's not coming anymore." The suddenness of his absence hurt. "I had hoped..."

"It is for the best." Mother said. "He's right. I think you are ready too."

"He won't make it to the audition."

"Why do you say that?"

"Just a feeling I have. The last time he was here, he acted differently...distant. I gave him the tickets, but he wasn't very excited about attending."

"Perhaps he realized things were coming to an end."

"No. It was more than that. We had...words. Plus, at the pub there is no one to take his place. His brother will help, but with his father ill it will be on Colin's shoulders to keep the business going. Thursdays are not always busy there, but with it being Valentine's Day, I know he won't be able to get away for my audition."

Mother walked to the wicker settee and sat down beside her. "I'm sorry, dear."

Gloria couldn't believe her. Her chest tightened with the thought. "Are you? Really? You never made him feel welcome here."

Mother pressed her lips together. "I know he is your...friend. And that is fine. But, Gloria, he isn't suitable for you as anything more than that."

"Suitable..." The words weighed on her, as they always had. "He makes me happy—without even trying. Like Tad. Like father."

"And George doesn't?"

"Not like Colin."

"George can give you things that Colin can't. That is more important. George will look after you."

"Like a child?" She was beginning to see things in a totally different light. "What do you think will happen if I am chosen in the competition, Mother?"

Mother arched her brow. "What do you mean? You will marry George. Once the audition is over, win or lose, I expect you to settle down...hopefully in that house just around the corner from here."

"So...you knew about that?"

"Didn't you mention it?" Mother asked innocently She averted her gaze and suddenly became interested in the arrangement of new lilies Clara had recently placed in the vase near her.

"No. Not once," Gloria said, watching her closely now.

"Well, perhaps George mentioned it in passing."

How much more did Mother know? Had George conspired with her to get Gloria to marry him? He was a master manipulator. Just look at how he'd pushed her by showing her that house. What had he discussed with Mother while Gloria concentrated on her music? Father wouldn't be involved too, would he? Father trusted George in business because of his shrewdness, but that didn't extend to personal matters. Father was not so gullible as that.

However, she was aware of one thing. She had never been completely sure which George wanted more—her or the Davis Shipping Company. Now, George was a business associate, but Father still held the balance of power in the company and could let him go if necessary with the same speed that he had fired Mr. Peers. If George married her, he would gain a permanent place in the company.

But did Mother and George's machinations even matter? By the way Colin had acted the last time he'd been at the house, he wasn't interested in her in any way that was more than a friend.

To think on it anymore made her tired...and numb. And that is what hurt beyond anything George or her mother might do. "I will be glad when this is over. I am looking forward to the audition, but I am heartily sick of practicing these two scores."

That evening after supper, Gloria went up to her room. At the foot of her bed, she knelt before her hope chest and withdrew the quilt Grandma Mary had made for her with the hope she would use it on her marriage bed. She remembered as a child seeing her grandmother work on many quilts over the years. *Idle hands are the devil's workshop* she had said more than once. Gloria smiled softly, staring for a moment at her own fingers caressing the soft material. She could hardly call her hands idle with all the music they made.

She spread the quilt over her bed and considered the pretty flower basket design of each square. As Grandma Mary worked on each one, she had said a special prayer just for Gloria and her intended — whoever that might be.

What she wouldn't give to talk to Grandma Mary right now — or even more — Tad. Her brother, more than anyone else, would help her figure out her own heart. He was good at that — cutting through her vague feelings to the crux of what was wrong. Oh how she missed him.

She smoothed her hand over the quilt. Stitched with love... After all the work Grandma Mary had put into it, how could she put this on a bed that would know no love? Because the truth was...she didn't love George and never could. The future that he envisioned was not the future she wanted for herself. She would never be right for him and that would eventually harm their marriage. Since she couldn't imagine George compromising at all, she would be the one to do so over and over until the urge to play her music would dry up and blow away. They would both end up bitter.

No matter how Colin might feel about her...he was the man who made her happy. When she thought of him—his smile, his warm laugh—something inside of her opened and breathed like a robin ready to take flight for the first time. He was the man she loved.

The next morning, Gloria helped her mother repot a few plants in the solarium before heading to the music room to practice. Clara was in the process of her weekly dusting, concentrating on the bust of Chopin, when Gloria entered the room. She immediately noticed Colin's satchel sitting on his chair.

"What's this?" she asked Clara.

"I found it while straightening the room, Miss. He must have left it behind the last time he was here. Would you like me to have Mr. Ross take it to him?"

And miss a chance to see Colin herself? She could find out for herself how his father was faring...how Colin was doing. Maybe she could take a small gift to the family to show that she was thinking of them in this difficult time. "I'll take care of it, Clara. Thank you."

She picked the satchel up, curious to see what was inside. Perhaps he still had one or two of his pub songs. Wouldn't that scandalize her mother if she warmed up with one of them? The thought brought a quick smile to her lips. Perhaps she should shut the door.

She waited for Clara to leave the room and then opened the folder and looked through the music pieces. Along with Heller's piece, Colin had also purchased Bach's Concerto No.3. On Bach's piece, Colin had written all over the score where she needed to be louder, softer, slower, faster. Where it was most difficult for her...and where she played it perfectly. As she had improved, he crossed out the words and at the end in big capital letters, he wrote the last three dates that he had been here and beside them the word—*PERFECT!* He'd put similar notations on the piece by Heller. Colin's validation meant more to her than any audition or competition.

She pulled out the song *Widdicombe Fair* and though she'd heard it before, she'd never played it. Sight-reading came easier than she expected. She played it through again.

She put aside *Where Did You Get That Hat?* and pulled out the loose pages behind it. They were written in Colin's own hand! Not store-bought music at all, but his very own. This didn't look like any of the other tunes he had written that he had played for her. Then she spotted the title up in the corner — *Gloria's Song*.

Intrigued, she spread it out on the piano stand and played the first few bars with one hand. It started out similar to *Canon in D* by Pachelbel, simple and sweet. In the next few bars, she added the left hand, stretching her fingers out over the keys. The tune became more complex, the mood intensifying. Before she knew it, she was playing it in earnest. There was only the music. The notes written in his hand on the paper absorbed into her as she read them and then flowed out through her fingers without conscious effort. The ending came in a huge, sweeping crescendo, reverberating throughout the room, before dropping to *pianissimo* for the last four measures in a quiet echoing of the first simpler strains.

She sat with her hand frozen on the keys — completely stunned. The song was sweeping, lush and romantic, the austere beginning only the tip of the movement. She had known Colin was good, but this — this went beyond that. *Colin had written this!* He had named this beautiful music that touched her very soul for her. The thought humbled her.

This came from his heart. For him to have written this, he had to feel something for her. The last time they had spoken, he had acted so distant, his words clipped and short. What had happened from the time he'd written this until then to change things? A tear slid down her cheek as she remembered his kiss. She wanted that feeling back. She wanted...him.

And it didn't matter that he lived on the other side of the trolley tracks. What he did, he did for love for his brother and parents. He put people first ahead of his music even though he had such a gift. She looked around the music room, bright with the wintry sun shining through the windows. It was cold. She had always put music first, even when she didn't want to, trying to please her mother and father. It was the one thing she did well and Mother didn't criticize. Perhaps, though, it was time to find a balance. Time to find her own place.

She played his music through from beginning to end again. And again.

CHAPTER FOURTEEN

The night before the audition a winter storm blew through that dropped six inches of new snow on the town. Colin was up early the next morning as he'd been the past ten days ever since his father had fallen ill, loading coal into the stove to take the chill off the rooms above the pub. While Ma prepared breakfast, he and James headed down the stairs without a word and grabbed the shovels to clear the snow off the steps and walkway.

"Will you be going to hear Miss Palmer today?" James asked.

"No."

"Why not?"

"It won't matter whether I'm there or not."

"You don't believe that. She gave you the tickets. And she came by the shop to leave your pay."

He'd been gone when she stopped in.

"I know she wanted to see you. She kept glancing about the pub until Ma mentioned you were gone, off to the docks to see about a shipment of ale."

He'd lied about that to Ma and Da. He'd actually stopped by Gunter's place to let Patrick know about Da.

"She wouldn't have done all that if she didn't want you there."

Colin had slept little, wrestling with the matter. He wanted to be there, but Welbourne's threat rang in his ears. If he came anywhere near Gloria, the man would call in Da's loan on the pub. Colin stopped working and leaned against his shovel. "A lot has happened since she handed me those tickets. I can't leave here. I've got too much to do."

"Well, you've been a real bear ever since you last saw her."

"We almost lost Da! Of course, I've been short."

"He's doing better now and you are still grouchy, so it's not all about Da and you know it."

"Just leave it!" He shoveled the last bit of snow on the walkway with a vengeance, the snow fairly flying off his shovel as he took his frustration out on it. He wanted to see Gloria's audition in the worst way. Yet he didn't want to jeopardize the pub.

"The conservatory is a public place. Welbourne can't keep you from going there." James cocked his head. "There ain't nothing that can't wait for a few hours and you'd be back in time to help with the busiest part of the evening. Maybe you'll hear from Patrick by then."

He knew James was trying to help, but Colin had to figure this out for himself. "I'll not let that Welbourne get his hands on this pub."

Ma knocked on the front window and motioned for them to come in for breakfast.

"Not a word to Ma about Patrick," Colin warned his brother as they stored their shovels in the corner behind the long bar. "She has enough on her mind with Da."

"He's getting better, stronger."

"I should have never been gone. It was my pride that got us into this mess," he muttered, shrugging out of his coat and then following James up the stairs to the apartment above. "I should have been here all along helping Da."

At the table, his father was sitting up. He waited while Colin and James took their seats.

"You're lookin' well, Da," Colin said.

"Now don't be changing the subject. I heard that last, Colin. And I won't have you blaming yourself for what happened to me. God alone knows the number of my days."

Ma sat down and he reached across the table to clasp her hand. "And I'll be livin' each of them fully."

"Now," he continued. "I've got something to say. But first, which one of you two took it upon yourself to speak to your cousin?"

How had Da found out? "It was me," he admitted, jutting up his chin. He wouldn't apologize. It had been time. Past time.

Da dropped his fist against the table. "I'm still the head of this house!"

They all jumped.

"Calm yourself, Shaun," Ma scolded. "Your temper is what caused the rift with Patrick in the first place. You're too important to me to be laid low again."

Da squeezed her hand. "Just so you know it," he continued, putting his other hand on Colin's shoulder. "I'm thinking you did the right thing, Boy-o…Colin. It's time to honor the blood between us and not the words spoken in haste. It's time I forgive my brother's boy."

"It's a good thing," Colin said. "He's family. When is he coming back?"

"Sometime today. I'm thinkin' if things work out, he might stay on longer." He took a spoonful of his porridge. "Maybe earn his share of the place."

James flashed Colin a wide grin. Then Ma and Da were grinning.

Breakfast was almost over when Colin mentioned the audition. He had to go. Even if just for half an hour. He had to hear Gloria play. "I'm going out today."

Da raised his bushy brows and then his blue eyes twinkled. "I wondered how long it would take for you to say something."

"What do you mean?"

"Miss Palmer mentioned her concert when she came by," Ma said. "While you were at the docks. She asked after you and James and Shaun too. She seems like a nice girl."

"It's not a concert. It's an audition," he said, staring at the packet.

"Even more important." Da looked Colin in the eye. "Your ma and I didn't know how to answer because you hadn't said a word about it."

"It is during our busiest time, Da. I wasn't planning to go. But…"

"Son, I hear the music you play late at night. An Irishman knows a love song when he hears it. It's plain to see you have feelings for her. She'll need your support today."

"She is all but promised to someone else. As soon as this is over, they'll be getting married."

Da sat back in his chair and rubbed his whiskered jaw. "So that's the way of it. I'm sorry to hear it."

Colin finished his breakfast and sat back too. He'd thought about Gloria constantly over the past ten days but that didn't mean he could figure out a way to be with her after this audition. They'd end up going their own way. They were simply from two different worlds.

"She worked hard," he said. "She deserves to win. And I want to be there when she does." He blew out a breath. "And it would be something to see the conservatory from the inside."

Ma and Da exchanged glances and then Ma smiled. "Then we'll depend on Patrick coming in time to help. You might want to stop by Rigetto's and buy a flower for her."

They were giving him their blessing.

It started snowing again on his way to the conservatory. He hunched against the wind, holding his scarf closed about his neck and, with his other hand checked for the tickets in his coat pocket. It wouldn't do to lose them. He strode through the main section of town, down the cobblestone streets. He stopped at Rigetto's and bought a single rose, tucking that inside his coat to keep it from freezing. Then he stopped in at Tamara's house and asked if she wanted to go with him. She was the one person he knew who might appreciate hearing the auditions. Together they crossed the wide street that circled and separated the conservatory's ten acres from the rest of Barrington and hurried up the brick walk to the front doors.

Most of the others had arrived and taken their seats by the time Colin had checked Tamara's coat and his own outer coat. The foyer to the auditorium had a marble floor and massive Grecian urns with greenery and lilies spilling out.

Tamara leaned near. "I feel like I should take off my shoes before walking on this! Colin, just imagine being a student here!"

They found two seats on the right side about halfway back from the stage. The way the ebony grand piano at the center of the stage stood, Gloria would be facing away from him on the bench.

He searched the auditorium for Welbourne and the Palmers, knowing that Gloria would be seated with them until she was called to perform. The thought amused him, remembering when she'd first asked him about his performance at the dinner club. He'd just considered it playing tunes. This today, was a bit more than that.

Welbourne and probably Gloria's mother would not want him here. They probably hoped he would not come.

The electric lights dimmed, with only the lights on the stage still bright.

Tamara smiled suddenly. "I see your Miss Palmer. She's there with her father and mother in the second row. I remember seeing them in the store a time or two. Oh, Colin! Just look at their fine clothes!"

He saw them now. Gloria leaned over to speak to her father. From this angle, he could see that she continually wrung her hands. She was either very nervous or her hands were cold. He remembered her saying that she couldn't play well with cold hands.

"I'll be right back," he told Tamara.

He strode up the aisle and straight to the coat check and asked for her muff.

"Who are you?"

"Miss Palmer's music tutor." He held out a coin.

The clerk gave over Gloria's muff.

"I'll take that." Welbourne snatched the muff from Colin. "I thought I told you not to bother her again."

"I'm not bothering her. I came to hear her performance."

Welbourne fished in his pocket and drew out a small jewelry box. He opened it to flash a gleaming gold and diamond ring. "I came prepared. And I expect you to continue to stay away once she is married. I still own the loan to McDougal's."

He didn't need the reminder about the pub. It was burned into his memory ever since he learned of it. "See that she gets her muff. I'm sure you don't want your future wife embarrassing you in front of all these people." Colin spun on his heel and headed into the auditorium before he said something stronger and caused a ruckus.

He took his seat and watched as Welbourne made his way down the aisle to sit on the other side of Mrs. Palmer. When Welbourne handed over the muff to Gloria, she stared at him, a curious look on her face, but immediately stuffed her hands inside it.

"You're back just in time," Tamara said. "It's starting. Your friend is fifth on the program."

They both settled back to listen. After his introduction, the first pianist took the stage amid polite applause. A tall, studious-looking man, he named the classic piece he would play and then sat down on the bench and began.

He would be a challenge to Gloria, Colin thought. But having never heard the music before, he wasn't sure if the man played it correctly. When he recognized only one of the sonatas after the next two pianists, he realized that he would be a very poor judge at something like this. Still, he enjoyed the music.

At the end of each piece, the five judges sitting on the stage, bent their heads and wrote furiously on their papers. The fourth was a girl younger than Gloria. One of the judges shook his head, already marking something down on his papers. After that, the girl's nervousness communicated itself to the audience and undermined her playing. There was an intermission when she finished.

Colin began to get his own case of nervousness that, in front of all these people, Gloria might react the same way the other woman had.

At that moment, Gloria stood and stretched, turning to scan the audience.

Tamara pressed close and whispered. "I think she is looking for you."

A judge on the panel, noticing her movement, motioned for her to come up on the stage. After a quick kiss on the cheek from her father, she headed up the steps to the side of the stage.

Colin couldn't take his gaze off her and imagined neither could any other man in the audience. She oozed confidence and gracefulness. Instead of wearing the traditional white blouse and black skirt women wore for performing during a concert, she had on a vivid royal-blue gown with a cinched waist and small bustle. The flowing sleeves draped from her elbow halfway down her dress, the black trim contrasting sharply with her skin. Her hair had been curled in a style that cascaded down her back to her waist.

She looked stunning.

Tamara nudged him. "I'm thinking that if her dress is any indication of her ability, then she is going to win."

He smiled, relaxing. "She's a corker."

She spoke for a moment with the judges and then stood back, waiting to be introduced. He could tell by the way she clasped her hands together, her fingers laced before her, that she was nervous, although only he would know that. To anyone else, she would appear poised and collected. Anticipation mounted inside him and he said a silent prayer for her.

Her dark gaze flickered over the audience as one of the judges made her introduction. She announced her first piece, the classical one by Bach, curtseyed and then sat back down at the piano. She adjusted her skirt, raised her hands to the keys, and began.

The music filled the room, sounding just the way she had practiced. He held his breath through the three difficult passages, but she played them, just as they were intended to be played. Colin looked over to see how the judges reacted. They would know this piece inside out and so her playing had to be impeccably precise. And…it was.

At the end, she rose and curtseyed again. And then she turned back to the piano.

"She forgot to announce Heller's piece," he said to Tamara. "I hope that doesn't take points off her score."

"Perhaps she is more nervous than we can tell from here."

His concern must have reached out to her, a tenuous thread over the heads of the audience members, for she looked out and tried to see beyond the lights, looking his way for a moment. Did she search for him? Did she know he was there for her? A tremulous smile appeared as she took a deep breath and turned away without finding him.

His chest tightened. If there was a way he could *will* her his confidence, *will* her his strength, he'd gladly do it.

She walked back to center stage.

"My last piece of music is one you have never heard before. It was written by a brilliant new composer, Colin McDougal. The name is *Gloria's Song.*"

Shocked at her words, Colin froze. She would sabotage her chances for entrance! Didn't she realize that? How could Gloria do this? She had worked so hard and now would give it up? Why? The judges would think he had pushed her to play his own music and that she had daftly gone along.

Welbourne rose halfway from his seat, an angry frown on his face as he searched the auditorium. He was probably looking for Colin. Finally, at Mrs. Palmer's touch to his sleeve, he sat down.

"Colin! Did you know?" Tamara asked in a hushed voice.

He shook his head. "She never practiced this. I didn't know she had it." He must have left it there the day James came for him about Da.

"I need to stop her." He stood and took two steps down the aisle, then hesitated. Would that only make things worse for her if he were to go up on stage? To create such a commotion would surely hurt her chances of winning even more. A part of him desperately wanted to hear his music played, here in this chamber of renowned music, and particularly by her. But he didn't want her ruining her own chances at her dream. She needed to win a placement. Only then would she finally grasp the gumption to refuse marriage to Welbourne. Until then, she couldn't see it as an option.

It was too late. She had already settled at the piano, her hands poised over the keys, waiting for the audience to quiet. The entire hall became silent, waiting. Colin stood there, transfixed as the achingly sweet music filled the hall. *His* music! She played the clear, singular sounds, then repeated them, letting them build until they became more complex, gripping the audience, gripping *him* with the power of her playing, the power of the music. On to the next transition and on further, her hands flew over the keys. She was unaware that every sound her fingers brought forth pulled at his heart and spoke to him more eloquently than if she'd spoken a word.

A lump formed in his throat, growing until he could scarcely breathe. She was telling him, without a word being spoken, that she loved him.

Slowly, he began to look about and take in the reactions of the audience and judges. No one moved or whispered. Gloria held them spellbound. When at last she played the final refrain and the last note hung in the air, sustained until it faded away into quiet, the audience sat transfixed. Colin held his breath, trying to gauge the mood in the room. One by one, people rose to their feet, clapping. Shouts of Bravo! Bravo! filled the room.

Gloria stepped to the front of the stage. She bowed and when she straightened, the beautiful smile on her face was made more beautiful by the glimmer of tears.

He walked down the aisle to the bottom of the steps and waited. The judges wrote on their papers and discussed among themselves in a way that told him Gloria had upended protocol. She noticed him standing there and stepped down the short set of stairs, taking his hand as she did.

"You came. I thought you were here…You knew that my hands were cold."

He nodded. "I knew. Of course I came. I couldn't stay away." He leaned closer and lowered his voice. "But I can't believe you did that! You crazy fool. You may have ruined your chances."

"It is beautiful, Colin. I couldn't play the other once I played this."

He reached up and wiped a tear from her cheek. He wanted to do more…he wanted to kiss her. "You shook everyone up."

She smiled. "Well, at least they weren't bored. We better sit down and let the auditions continue." She glanced to the row of seats where her parents sat. "It looks like George has left an empty seat for you."

He shook his head. "Tamara came with me. She wanted to hear you too."

"Or she wanted to hear your music."

"Neither one of us knew what you were up to. Oh…" He reached inside his jacket and pulled out the rose, offering it to Gloria. He wanted to say so much, but not here in this crowded room. "You don't have to worry about her."

She accepted the flower. Her green eyes shined. "And you don't have to worry about Welbourne."

"Does that mean—"

"If everyone would take their seats, we will continue," a judge interrupted from the stage.

"We will talk afterwards," Colin whispered, and gave her a quick kiss on the cheek.

CHAPTER FIFTEEN

That kiss tingled on her cheek long after they separated and she made her way back to her seat. It blazed a trail inside right to her heart, which was already so full she could barely breathe. She tried to concentrate on the following performances, but failed utterly.

When the next pianist began, George returned to his seat beside her. He gave no excuse as to why he'd been gone, but she could feel anger radiating off him as if it were heat. She wondered why he had come back at all.

After all the pianists had performed, Gloria gathered in the foyer of the auditorium with her family and George and waited to hear the decisions of the judges. They were expected within the hour. The other pianists did the same. On the far side of the hall, Joseph Peers, who had played in the next-to-last spot, stood beside his father.

Colin and Tamara approached.

"Mr. McDougal," Father said, turning to him. "That didn't sound like *La Favorita.*"

"No, sir. No, it didn't. I was as surprised as you."

"Come now. You had to know…"

"No, Father," she answered. "He truly didn't know. When he dashed out of the house upon learning his father had collapsed, he left his music folder. Clara came across it while dusting the room and gave it to me."

Father's lips twitched. "So, you pilfered it."

"And practiced it like a madwoman," she admitted.

"You took quite a risk." His eyes shone with pride. "It is something I might have done"—he cleared his throat— "in my youth."

She met Colin's gaze. It wasn't such a risk at all. His music should be heard. She turned her focus to George. There was, however, one outcome she was already sure of, and she didn't need an announcement from the judges to know her mind.

"George. May I speak with you a moment? Privately?"

A shadow of misgiving crossed his expression. He knew what was coming. He took her aside to an alcove, keeping them both within view of the rest of the assembly. Yet, with her back to the wall, it seemed he positioned himself as a barrier. "You are making a mistake, Gloria," he said, his tone low and insistent.

"I don't believe that I am."

"You are not thinking straight."

She couldn't let him sway her. Not this time. "I am sorry it hasn't work out as you planned. Your persistence has been flattering, George, and I appreciate you waiting as my father requested. It was wise…for the both of us. These weeks that I've had to wait, I have come to realize that I am not the right woman for you."

He took a deep breath and then exhaled slowly. "Is it McDougal?"

"No." She looked down for a moment to prepare her words. "It is me. Music is my passion...my gift from God. I don't want to deny it or hide it away. I want to honor it. I want to honor *Him* with it."

"We could work something out..."

"No, George. Either you would be unhappy...or I would. I want a different future than you do. One that is centered around my music and around people who understand that part of me."

"People like McDougal?" He sneered as he said the name. "You believe he understands you? He can't offer you anything. All he's done is turn your head."

She took a firmer stance. "This is about me and my music. Not Colin."

"He'll pay," George said, his look dark.

A sliver of worry trembled through her. Her decision wasn't about Colin. She had to make George understand. "You are not hearing me!"

"Oh, I hear you fine. I just don't believe you." His eyes narrowed.

She remembered how formidable he could be. How calculating. Fear for what he might do to Colin twisted in her chest. "What do you mean, he'll pay?" she asked carefully.

He lifted his chin, looking down his nose at her. "I hold the lien to the tavern his family works. Could be I need the cash. Could be I need to call in that debt."

She pulled back. "I can't believe you said that! My decision has little to do with Colin. It has to do with me!"

"I don't like to lose. You should know that by now."

She drew in a sharp breath.

"Don't do this, Gloria. I could give you so much. You'd never want for anything. We are good together."

She closed her eyes to shut out the appeal in his. In the past, she had been swayed by such arguments. To be accepted, to gain approval, had been her main desire. Yet this was too important a decision for her to just settle. "I can't go back. I won't," she said softly, but with a firmness beneath the words. She met his gaze.

She pitied him. He had no comprehension of the joy music could bring. It wasn't in him. To live a life without music would crush her. She looked down at her muff, gathering her thoughts to say the one thing he had to hear. It had to be said. She met his gaze. "Whether I am selected tonight to go to the conservatory or not, I must decline your offer of marriage. And should you, in any way, approach the McDougal family regarding their loan, I will do all that I can to see that my father pays it off and that you are left in need of new employment."

He stared at her for a long moment, his expression grave. Then he walked to the coat man, took his overcoat and top hat, and left.

She let out a sigh. It was over. That part of her life was behind her. She turned to rejoin her parents and found, that although Colin was standing with them, his focus was on her.

"Is everything all right?" he asked, as she approached.

The concern in his blue eyes warmed her. With him she felt secure, but it had nothing to do with money. He understood her and he loved her. They spoke the same language. "It is now," she said. "I declined his marriage offer."

"Here?" Mother said, aghast, her hand splayed across her chest. "Gloria, you didn't!"

"The waiting period is officially over. There was no point in putting it off. He had a right to know how I felt."

"This was all your doing, Stephen!" Mother said. "Now look what has happened."

Father regarded her steadily. "What has happened, is that our daughter has made up her mind what is most important for her happiness."

"Well…" Mother sputtered. "Well…" she said, less certain now.

Gloria turned to her father. "You knew all along what would happen, didn't you? That's why you insisted on the waiting period."

"I didn't know what outcome you would chose. I only knew that once I met your mother, there was no way I was going to let her get away. And, if she will think back, she will remember that she felt the same way toward me." He reached down and squeezed Mother's hand. "When Welbourne offered for you, I didn't see that spark in your eyes. Instead, you hesitated. A woman in love doesn't do that. I had to know that when I gave you away in marriage, that there would be no doubts, no regrets. When you chose to marry, you must be absolutely sure that is what you want beyond all else."

"So...you expect me to wait for love to come along?" She couldn't help looking at Colin. He returned her gaze steadily.

Just then, a judge stepped out from the closed room where the others had been deliberating. The assembly quieted and all eyes focused on the man speaking.

"All the pianists that auditioned were accomplished musicians in their own right. The decision process was not an easy one. But we have now come to our decision regarding the three students we would like to invite to enter the conservatory at the start of the spring season."

Gloria held her breath and strained to hear so as not to miss a word. Everything she hoped for hinged on the next few seconds. She felt Colin take her hand and squeeze it. Gratefulness that he was here, next to her, spilled over her.

"Armand More. Lawrence Sutton. Gloria Palmer."

The assemblage erupted into cheers.

Colin hugged her, but then suddenly disappeared as her mother, her father, and other people she barely knew came up to hug and congratulate her. Mr. More and Mr. Sutton introduced themselves and congratulated her. They spoke at length of what would be expected of her in the coming months—a spring concert and then a tour through the summer to New York City and Chicago. She was thrilled at the itinerary they dangled before her. Her excitement was tempered only by the knowledge that she would miss Colin during her time away.

Each time a different instructor from the conservatory approached and spoke of another engagement they had planned for her, Mother would struggle against tears. "It's just so much to take in," she said, dabbing at her eyes with her handkerchief. "Will I ever see you?"

Colin, Gloria suddenly realized, was no longer at her side. As the crowd melted toward the doors to leave, she searched the room for him. Had he left without saying goodbye? It didn't seem possible. Tamara, also, was nowhere in sight.

"It's time we headed home," Mother said. "The day has been eventful and we have a lot to talk about. There are new plans to make."

Father helped them with their cloaks and they walked to their waiting carriage. All the while, Gloria looked for Colin, hoping to see him before she left. When they were settled in the carriage and on their way, Gloria couldn't help but feel everything was anticlimactic. She had wanted to share this time with Colin. It was his night too.

"What's wrong?" Father asked.

"Oh, nothing," she said, as brightly as she could. "I...I guess I hoped that Colin would celebrate with us a bit longer. After all, it was his music piece that helped me win."

"I see," Father said seriously, looking from her to Mother. "In that case, perhaps a slight detour is in order." He wrapped his cane on the roof of the carriage.

Mr. Ross turned the coach down the next side street. How did he know where Father wanted to go? "Father?"

He merely smiled.

A few moments later, they stopped in front of McDougal's Pub.

The place was alight with business. Through the front window, an assortment of men stood at the bar and more men crowded around a front table.

"Stephen! You can't be serious!" Mother said. "A tavern?"

"Oh, I am, Mrs. Palmer. This is Gloria's night...and Mr. McDougals."

"Well, I've had enough excitement for one day. I am not getting out of this coach."

"I wouldn't expect anything less, dear." He stepped to the curb and then turned to Gloria. "Mind you, daughter. I won't have you frequenting a pub either. Wait here and I'll see if I can find your young composer."

He disappeared into the colorful hubbub of men inside. Gloria strained to see through the open coach door. It seemed an eternity later that Colin came out of the tavern. He had doffed his coat and now wore only the pants and shirt that she had always seen him. His shirtsleeves were rolled up to his elbows and he looked as though he had spent the evening as usual, working away in the tavern. He didn't seem to notice the cold, although a mist rose with every breath he took walking toward her. He only had eyes — and a big grin — for her.

She felt the same way.

"This reminds me of the first time I met you, Miss Palmer."

"A lot has changed since that night."

He turned to her mother. "Mr. Palmer will be out directly. He is speaking with my da. I'd like a moment to speak with Gloria. With your permission."

He barely gave Mother a chance to answer, before he opened the carriage door and held out his hand for Gloria. He pulled her a few feet away.

"You left so suddenly after the announcement," she said. "I looked everywhere for you."

"Did you, now?" He took her hands in his, a half-smile on his face. "You missed me then?"

His easy manner surprised her. Although Gloria faced away from her mother and the coach, she knew Mother must be watching closely. Colin didn't seem to care. "What happened that you left so suddenly?"

"One of the judges took me aside. They wanted permission to publish *Gloria's Song*. We are meeting about it tomorrow."

"Oh Colin! That's wonderful! It is what you have wanted."

He grinned. "Well, I thought when Tin Pan Alley took notice of my music it would be for a tune a person could dance to or sing, not something classical."

She smiled. "It's neither. Your music is in a class all its own. It's romantic and lush and beautiful."

"And it's yours."

"No, Colin. I'll accept my name on it and am grateful for that, but it is your music. Yours."

The lights through the pub window, sparkled in his eyes. They darkened as he studied her. "Guess I can't hide that you were my inspiration."

Heat suffused her cheeks. She'd never been anyone's inspiration before.

"There's more."

"More? How can this night get any better?"

He took her hands in his. "They offered me a position at the conservatory. I'm to compose and work with the graduate students."

Her heart was near to bursting! Colin—at the school with her! It seemed too good to be true. "What did you say? What did you decide?"

He swallowed. "Well. I had to come speak to my father and make sure he could keep the pub going without me. That's why I left without a proper goodbye to you."

"And…?" She was impatient to hear all the news.

"Apparently, my cousin, Patrick is quite willing to take my place here. He and James can handle it. My da didn't even so much as blink when I mentioned the offer."

"So…you will say yes tomorrow at the meeting?"

He looked down at their hands, clasped together. "I'll take the position only if I can continue working with you. There are more songs I want to write. And you are my inspiration."

"Oh, Colin…"

"As a matter of fact, I asked if I would be touring with you."

She hadn't thought that far ahead. All this was so much to take in. "What did they say?"

"They said…that would work best if we were married."

Had she heard correctly? He hadn't said that he loved her, but she saw his love shining in his eyes and she heard it in the music he'd written for her. She could barely contain herself. She threw her arms around him, hugging him right there in the middle of the walkway. Behind her, Mother gasped, but Gloria didn't care. Let her see. Let anybody see. The news was too wonderful to be still and proper.

A surprised second passed and then his hands gripped her waist and slid around to encircle her, drawing her tight to him. Through his cotton shirt, she could feel his heart thudding a rhythm against her cheek and the tickle of his breath on her forehead. If only she could stay right here forever. She was content. She was happy. And she was in love.

Colin stroked her hair away from her temple. "I take it you agree."

"Very much so. I am fairly bursting with joy."

He pulled back slightly, the pleased look on his face growing serious. "It wouldn't have happened without you, Gloria. I owe this to you."

"Oh no, Colin!" She had to protest. They'd helped each other. It had been a true partnership. "You don't owe me anything. It's the same as you told me. You have a gift. One for the world to know."

He chuckled, the sound low and rumbling. "I do at that. And she's right here in my arms."

Then he leaned down and kissed her. Tenderly… magically… completely…

Thank you for reading Gloria's Song!
If you enjoyed this book, please help other
readers find it by leaving a review. Just a few
words will do. Reviews make *all* the difference!

Enjoy the romances of my character's (Gloria's)
siblings and cousins. Every title is a Clean, Sweet
Western Historical Romance.
To learn more about our series and the
individual books, visit the Sweet Americana
Amazon Page.

.

ABOUT THE AUTHOR

Kathryn Albright writes American-set historical romance ~ Westerns for Harlequin Historical and now Gloria's Song, which is her first eastern setting. Her stories celebrate courage and hope with a dash of adventure. Kathryn's stories have been finalists in the distinguished RWA Golden Heart® and the HOLT Medallion as well as several other industry contests. She enjoys road trips with her husband (when he drives) and being caught up in a good story. She currently lives with her family in the rural Midwest.

Find out more about Kathryn and her books at www.KathrynAlbright.com. She is also active on social media on Facebook, Twitter, and Pinterest.